STAINED GLASS ROSE

Stained Glass Rose

A Historical Novel

D. A. BROCKETT

To Mary - enjoy the story. Blessings! DABrockett

WESTERN REFLECTIONS PUBLISHING COMPANY®

Montrose, CO

This book is a work of fiction, though based partially on real events and people from 1937 Grand Junction. Unless noted in the final chapter or in the acknowledgments, all names, places, characters and events either are products of the author's imagination or are used fictitiously. Any other resemblance to actual events, or locales, or persons living or dead is entirely coincidental.

First Edition
Printed in the United States of America

Library of Congress Catalog Card Number 2002101584

ISBN 1-890437-61-1

Cover and text design by Laurie Goralka Design

Western Reflections Publishing Company®
P.O. Box 1647
Montrose, CO 81402
www.westernreflectionspub.com

This book is dedicated to the memory of
Jeanette Morris
and to her son,
Fred Rule

Acknowledgements

No book is written by one person. I have so many people to thank, not only for their contributions to the story, but their encouragement to write *Stained Glass Rose*. Please forgive me if I forget anyone — it has taken me three years to set this story to print. Hopefully, you will find a bit of yourselves nestled among the words of this book.

First of all, if my husband, Ben, had not believed in me, provided the time, materials, editing, and encouragement for me, this book would never have been written. Thank you, sweetheart.

Next, to Steve Henderson, husband of my twin, Robyne, thank you for the tens of hours you put in to edit my book and encourage me. Your insight was invaluable. Thanks, Robbie, for sharing him.

To Karen O'Connor of Sparrow Perch Studios (970-245-4254), thanks for designing the stained glass panel for my book. It is truly beautiful, like you.

To Peggy Godfrey, a lovely poet, who lent me my favorite poem of hers, *God Has Been The Woman*. Thanks for encouraging me to, "live all the way out to the edge of my skin."

To Western Slope Christian Writers Association members, who wrote, called, or spoke your encouragement over the years — thank you. This means you, Maxine Bamburg, Sharon Bridgewater, Karen Brownlee, Shirley Ewing, Beverly Heirich, Muriel Morley, Heidi Nichols, Terri Patoine Hanson, Linda Simpson, and others. A special thanks to Linda Beckley, Dennis Curry, Rusty Morgan and Ursala Vogt for your tremendous critiques.

To the board of WSCWA, thank you Steve (again), Lynda Munfrada, Merilyn Ferris, and Ginger Millermon, who played a big part in my writing career.

Thank you, Torry Martin, for the joke. I think of you every time I read it.

And a special thanks to Tom Trujillo, who believed in me and, for six years, allowed me the pleasure of writing for his magazine, *The Testimony*.

As for contributors to the story, a big thanks to historian, Dave Fishell, for the interesting hours of conversation on his front porch; to Mesa County Coroner, Rob Kurtzman, who listened to my questions and offered professional insight, to Glenna Sheley, of the Grand Junction Police Department, who was excited enough about SGR to send me information about the Apron String Murder and Mrs. Jennie Ward, and let me peruse through dusty ledgers to see what I could find. Thanks to Chris Franz of the Mesa County Sheriff's Department, who shared crime scene realities, and was available for any questions I had; to Judy Prosser-Armstrong and Sissi Williams of the Museum of Western Colorado, who took me in and nurtured my quest with encouragement, facts, and love. A special thanks to Alice Else, Harold Daniels, Ivan Crick, Marjorie Jones, Dr. Roland Marasco, and Lorraine Williams for their interviews. So much of what they told me about life in Grand Junction in the 1930s sculpted the story.

Thanks to Dave Sundal for telling me about the Hotel D'Hamburger and Olive Blackburn. Thank you, Doralyn Genova for lending your wonderful aunt to SGR.

Although most of the characters are fictitious or are composites, I want to thank several people who let me use true parts of themselves. Thanks to Ivan Crick, Jr., Marjorie Penberthy Jones, Hazlett Wubben, and Lorraine Arcieri Williams — all members of the 1939 Graduating Class of Grand Junction High School. Thanks to Father Aloysius Bertrand, nephew of Father Nicholas Bertrand, for letting me put a bit of both men into the character of Father Nick. Thanks to Georgia Munro for introducing me to Dr. E.E.H. Munro, a legendary man and incredible doctor.

A big thanks goes to Roland and Rae Marasco for their encouragement and detailed information about Little Italy and Italian life.

Thank you, P. David Smith, publisher of Western Reflections Publishing, for your encouragement.

Thank you Dick Jones, Thelma Liggett, May Bourne, and Fred Rule for sharing Jeanette with me and the world.

Last of all, thank you dear Lord, for giving me a talent and a passion to make a difference.

GOD HAS BEEN THE WOMAN

By Peggy Godfrey

God has been the woman
Who comforts me when no one else is near, when pain is so
sharp, breathtaking
that I can't even say where it hurts.
Sings me lullabies during nights when I can't rest
Holds me gently in Her vast silence when I need
gentleness and quiet.
God has been the woman
Who takes my hand and leads me from girlhood
to womanhood.
Holds the mirror as I readjust the image of
who I thought I was — to who I am.
Who midwifes my dreams, cuddles my creations,
coaxes me to try
new recipes for everything.
God is the woman
Who builds little fires in the cold rooms to warm me
To the idea of living all the way out to the edge of my skin.

Prologue

Smoke tinged the night air as the 1936 Packard hummed over the bridge. Underneath, the Colorado River drifted leisurely, winding westward toward Utah. A light breeze blew through the open windows of the car, but barely cooled the interior.

Nick Archieri couldn't remember a hotter summer. San Jose was bad enough, but the Western Slope of Colorado was stifling, as distant wildfires sprinkled soot on the picturesque valley that cradled Grand Junction, Fruita, Clifton and Palisade. The air was so dry, Nick could almost hear his eyelids blink. He hoped their visit would be short.

The glint of his wedding band caught his eye, and he felt his throat constrict with a sudden surge of agony. The first anniversary of Katharine's death was approaching, and Nick wasn't sure he'd make it. He dragged his eyes toward his grandmother's comforting profile. At the moment, Nonna was the only thing keeping him from following his wife.

He reached into his pocket and fingered the bottle of pills he'd carried with him since the funeral. A week ago, he'd poured them out on the kitchen counter and had just set a large glass of water next to them, when the doorbell rang.

Nonna had stood on the porch, regally leaning against her walker. With his grandmother, one never had to guess what she was thinking. Her eyes sparkled in humor, snapped in anger, squinted in distrust, or softened in affection. That day, they were commanding, and no one ignored Rose Marie Archieri when she looked like that.

His grandmother had stated that a "long overdue obligation" needed to be taken care of, and he was to drive her to Colorado. Immediately.

His miserable life had been saved — for the moment. Nick glanced at his grandmother again and felt his agony dissolve into affection.

A red pillbox hat sat squarely above short salt and pepper hair, and a matching cashmere sweater enshrouded her frail shoulders. Nonna was fastidious about her clothing and always dressed well — even when visiting cemeteries in the dead of night, Nick thought with a grimace.

In the moonlight, Nonna's dark, intelligent eyes eagerly absorbed the ghostly scenery. Nick could tell his grandmother was enjoying her late-night adventure.

"Turn here, Nicky, and follow that road past the first gate."

Nick drove by an arched iron entrance, inserted in a long, low stone wall. The engine's drone waxed and waned as they passed several more arches.

"I think it's at the crest of this hill," Rose said, her tapered hands fluttering above her lap. Her voice, though thin with age, still sounded melodious and rich. Any remnants of an Italian accent had been lost in her youth.

"Are you sure we should be doing this, Nonna?"

"There, by that elm. My goodness, it was a sapling the last time I saw it!" Before the car came to a full stop, she pulled at the door handle.

"Let me help, Nonna," Nick said. "You'll hurt yourself."

"Uffa! I'm not as weak as you think."

His grandmother leaned against the Packard's shiny black fender, while he reached in and retrieved her walker and a folded lawn chair from the back seat.

Shortly after Katharine's death, Nonna had insisted her vintage car needed restoration. Rusting in her garage for as long as he could remember, he doubted the Packard was serviceable, but one didn't question Nonna, at least not to her face. Besides, a diversion was needed. He'd towed it to his garage and was surprised when the engine started right up. The old car displayed a tenacious spirit. Perhaps some of his grandmother had rubbed off on the mohair seats, he'd thought. This trip to Colorado was the renovated car's maiden voyage.

Nick walked beside his grandmother, as she made her way to the tree. He unfolded the chair, kicking a small rock away to level it. The full moon glistened on the nearby gravestones, while, at Nonna's feet, the elm's branches provided a carpet of mottled shade.

"Ah, Nicky, I thought I'd never return to this place. And now," a deep sigh escaped, "here I am." The chair barely creaked, as her weight

settled onto the weave. She looked around her. "I learned to drive in this place." Rose chuckled when she saw her grandson's stricken face.

"Don't look so shocked. It wasn't my idea; it was Mari's." Her voice became a caress. "She could make you do things you'd never dream of doing yourself."

Huh, like someone else I know. Nick cringed as he peered into the darkness. How would they explain this to the police if they were seen?

"Stop hovering, young man, and go get it." As Nick opened the trunk, she called, "Bring a flashlight, too. You'll need to find the grave. My eyes are weak."

"Nonna, shouldn't we at least whisper?"

Nick lifted a heavy bundle, wrapped in burlap, from the trunk and carefully laid it on the grass near his grandmother's feet. He made a second trip to the car for a shovel and small duffel bag.

"The summer I left hadn't been as hot as this one, Nicky, but a warm spring had provided the best crop of Palisade peaches in years. Their heady scent filled the valley from Palisade to the red cliffs in the west. Jobs were still scarce, but the bumper crop seemed a sign the lean times were almost over." She smacked her lips. "I can almost taste their sweetness in my mouth."

Ignoring the rumble of his stomach, Nick zipped up his coveralls and pulled on leather gloves. He was ready to get this deed over with.

"I think it's near there, Nicky."

He searched the scruffy ground and within minutes he'd found the spot. The woody sentinel towering over them amplified metal striking dirt.

"There were so many questions that summer of 1937. Why did the Hindenburg crash? Would they find Amelia Earhart? Would the Junction Tigers go to state again? The most important question for me was, would Papa ever love me? You see, my father, your great-grand-father, Nicky, had had a terrible problem and, that summer, it nearly destroyed us both."

Chapter One

A truck, careening around the corner, narrowly missed Rose, as she scooted onto the curb. Black lettering on the door stated, "Joe's Auto Repair." Rose resisted the urge to thumb her nose at the retreating vehicle. *Traffic these days,* she groused. *Grand Junction is getting too big for its bridges.*

Rose giggled at her pun and felt a spring return to her step as she walked toward St. Joseph Catholic Church. The farther she got from her house, the happier she felt.

She carefully detoured around the two-block area nicknamed Shantytown, where prostitutes lived and conducted business.

Like any semblance of sin, good Italian girls avoided this area. A young lady's determination to remain pure in thought, word and deed, however, wasn't helped when such spectacular sin resided just around the corner from Little Italy.

Was it only Rose who struggled with temptation? She tried to be a good girl — she really did. Even if Papa had a differing opinion. Despite what her father thought, most of the time she felt she succeeded in her mission. Of course, there were times when she failed miserably. One incident stood out in her mind, and only she, Father Nick, and the good Lord above knew about it.

One summer night, Rose had been overcome with curiosity about Shantytown. Peeking around the corner of the New World Restaurant, she'd seen bawdy women leaning against doorjambs. They'd waved at the schoolboys cruising by, and the boys had waved back, honking enthusiastically. Some of them had even stood up in their rumble seats, trying to catch forbidden sights in the lighted windows.

Goons, she'd sniffed, but couldn't help grinning at their antics. Then, she'd seen her own father slink from a doorway and head toward the tracks.

There were reasons good Italian girls minded the rules. Running home, Rose had prayed she wouldn't die before confession that week. To cover her bases, she'd imposed on herself five *Hail Marys* and threw in two *Our Fathers* for good measure.

Since then, she strictly avoided Shantytown.

Striding down Main Street, Rose passed businesses boasting Italian names: Raso, Fuoco, Grasso. She was proud of her heritage, and how the immigrants had made a place for themselves in Beloved America.

A flash of color at Rush-Sanford Clothiers caught her attention, and the girl stopped to gaze in the window. A yellow dress with white polka dots was displayed attractively, while next to it hung the red version. Both were priced at three dollars.

She focused on her reflection in the glass, picturing each dress in place of her Salvation Army frock. She pulled her bodice so the bruise at the base of her neck was hidden. Flipping her thick braid over one shoulder, she wished for the millionth time that Papa would let her bob her hair, like her school friends. Papa insisted good Italian girls kept their hair long, and she never dared to question Papa. At least not to his face.

Rose had darker looks than most of her classmates. She didn't mind. She was proud of her large expressive eyes, tiny waist, and graceful hands. Why, she'd even caught Ivan, the right tackle on Junction's football team, admiring her ankles in the school halls.

Rose felt the weight of coins sewn into the hem of her sleeve. Perhaps, Ivan would find her ankles even more attractive below a new dress.

She sighed. *What's the use of dreaming?* She knew she couldn't spend one penny. Tomorrow was Papa's birthday, and she might need all her secret money for his present.

Her ancestors hadn't celebrated birthdays in the old country, but she loved the great American tradition. Unfortunately, Papa followed the old ways, and Rose's seventeen birthdays had passed without a hint of acknowledgment.

She heard delicate laughter behind her and saw a small group of well-dressed young ladies, arms laden with packages, reflected in the window. They were smiling at her and whispering. Turning around, Rose thought they were the prettiest women she'd ever seen. One, whose auburn hair framed her face in soft curls, reached out and caressed Rose's cheek with a manicured finger.

"The red would go better with your complexion, little one." Her voice sounded like warm honey on hot rolls.

"You shouldn't, Darla." One of the ladies held out an admonishing hand.

A horn tooted nearby. Rose saw her friend, Marj, driving past in her beat-up old Chevy, Agony. With its numerous dents and chipped paint, Rose had always thought the moniker perfect. Despite the flivver's dubious looks, it was reliable, and that's what counted these days. Rose waved and when she looked back, the group of ladies was crossing the street. Darla winked over her shoulder.

In a million years, I'll never look that glamorous. Rose watched them stroll for a minute more, then turned toward St. Joe's.

After spending the morning polishing pews, Rose walked to the park to eat her dinner. She lowered herself into the shade of an elm tree. Coming from the direction of the soup kitchen, a delicious aroma of fresh bread and homemade vegetable soup enveloped her.

The Catholic sisters daily served numerous hobos and unemployed men in the valley, no questions asked. Rose had stopped by one time, but quickly decided it would be her last visit. The food was delicious, but the stench of poverty was overwhelming. She did not know how the sisters endured. It surely earned them some points in Heaven.

Tucking her feet under her dress, she unfolded her handkerchief and spread it flat on the grass. An apricot, a thick slab of bread and thin slices of salami were withdrawn from the pockets of her skirt, unwrapped and placed neatly in the middle of the starched white square. Nearby, several laughing children chased each other around their mother, who was laying out a picnic lunch.

Rose felt a pang of envy. She'd never known her mother.

She bowed her head, crossed herself and murmured a blessing. *Bless us O Lord, and these thy gifts, which we are about to receive . . . .* When she lifted her head, Rose was startled to realize she was no longer alone.

The young man's blue eyes were friendly above a shy smile, and pale freckles spanned the bridge of his slightly crooked, swollen nose. In spite of the swelling, Rose noticed he was on the handsome side. She guessed he was a little younger than she, around fifteen or sixteen. As he ran a tentative hand through wavy, dark hair, her glance took in his soiled coveralls and threadbare work shirt.

His glance fell to her meal.

She pointed toward the church. "The soup kitchen's that way."

Freckles blurred, as the young man nodded vigorously, but instead of heading off in the direction of the church, he sat down next to her. His movements were akin to a pocketknife folding into itself — precise and graceful.

Placing his worn hat between them, he said, "Name's Satter Simpson. What's yours?"

Good Italian girls didn't engage in conversation with strangers, especially if the stranger was a rude young man. Rose looked at the nearby family and wondered if she should join them. No, she really didn't want to impose. Sighing, she looked back at her unexpected visitor. He seemed safe enough. Besides, there was bound to be a story behind that nose.

"My name is Rose. Like the flower." She held out her hand, which was engulfed in a large, calloused grip.

His reply sounded something like, "Mawty nawsta meecha."

It took a moment for Rose to decipher what she'd heard. *Mighty nice to meet you.* She nodded, knowingly. Not a local but, she mentally shrugged, who was these days?

Satter's eyes fell downward again, so she tore her bread in half, topped it with three slices of salami, and offered it to her new acquaintance.

She smiled, as he chewed animatedly, his enjoyment obvious. She ate too, and when Satter eyed the apricot, she held it out to him.

"You were hungry! Did you just pull into town?"

Another blur of freckles. "Left the railroad couple of days ago. Was gandy-dancing. Eastern Utah."

Between sentences, Satter licked the fruit's juice that ran down his hand. Rose handed him her handkerchief. He sopped at his hands and mouth before returning it. It had soaked up more dirt than juice.

"What's candy dancing?"

He grinned broadly. *"Gandy*-dancing. After Gandy Manufacturing Company of Chicago. They used to make railroad tools, but they went belly-up."

"You dance with tools?"

Satter chuckled. "Dames!"

Rose's cheeks, and temper, began to flare. She jumped up. "Well, if you're not going to explain — "

"Hey, don't get sore." He patted the ground. "Didn't mean to offend you."

Rose sniffed, but settled herself on the grass again, giving him a warning look.

Satter grinned back. "Why, even spittin' mad, you're cute." He lifted his hand to calm her renewed indignation. "Now, hold your fire, young lady. Let's get back to the matter at hand." He cleared his throat.

"Gandy-dancers help lay railroad tracks," he said, as if reciting a passage he'd memorized from a manual. "They follow the jack crews, tamping gravel or slag into the raised space under each tie. It's called 'dancing' 'cause the long line of workers all move together, like they's doing a crazy dance." Satter crooked an arm, and a large muscle pressed against his shirtsleeve. "You can see, that kind of work ain't for Milquetoasts."

Rose stared at the bulge, and felt her heart skip. *Get a hold of yourself, for goodness sake!* She dragged her eyes upward. "My papa works for the railroad."

"Yeah? Doing what?"

"He works in the roundhouse. Like most everyone in my neighborhood."

"A steady job. That's good. Me, I've had it with the railroad. Damn hard work, er, 'scuse me, *dern* hard work dancing ten hours a day, nearly every dad-blasted day of the week." He reached up and pulled on a low tree branch. "No shade, neither, for miles and miles."

He looked at Rose, pointedly. "Seems I got *three* good reasons to stick around town a bit longer." The branch snapped upward.

Rose felt a flutter in her belly and began folding her handkerchief to cover her confusion. "Three?"

"Hmm?"

"You said you had three reasons."

"Oh. Yeah, my sister lives here, too. She'd like me to stick around for a while. Says she misses me. Heard J.C. Penney's was hiring, so maybe I'll apply for the position there."

Silently, Rose hoped he got the job, but these days, married men usually got first crack at any available openings.

"You live near here?" Satter gazed around the park.

"No, mornings I work at St. Joseph Catholic Church." She looked affectionately in the direction of the church. "Everyone calls it 'St. Joe's' for convenience's sake." Leaning against the tree trunk, she pointed toward the south end of town. "I live that way, down by the railroad. Little Italy."

"You don't sound Eye-talian."

Rose replied, "My parents were immigrants from Italy, but," she raised her chin in pride, "I was born here in America. Where are you from?"

"Oklahoma. Folks moved here a few years back, and now Pa's a sharecropper out Fruitvale way. Everyone's crammed in a three room boxcar on the property." The boy chuckled. "You can't miss the place. Leaning against the outdoor privy is a scarecrow that looks like Eleanor Roosevelt dressed in britches. Pa don't care for opinionated womenfolk, you see."

"Ah. He sounds like *my* father." Papa's stern face flashed in Rose's mind, but she brushed the image away quickly. "You said 'crammed.' How many people live there?"

"My folks and five of the kids. Oh, yeah, and my nephew lives there, too."

"My goodness, they must feel like sardines!"

Satter's brows came together. "Room enough for everyone but yours truly, it seems, even though it was me who helped Pa tend the fields that first year. After harvest, he kicked me out on my own."

"Why don't you still work with him?"

He winced as he touched the tip of his nose. "Matter of fact, yesterday I approached him 'bout that very idea, but he didn't take kindly to my inquiry." His jaw became hard. "See, Pa thinks I'm worthless. But, I'm gonna show him! One day he'll see what I'm made of!"

Rose placed a calming hand on his and said, "I'm sure you'll make him proud." She decided to change the subject. "Satter, if you don't live with your parents, where do you live?"

The young man's voice still held an edge when he answered. "Don't got a real home. My sister lives in town, and I sometimes stay with her, but most times, my home is wherever I lay my head."

Rose thought of the little house she shared with Papa. No matter how hard she tried, she could never make it feel warm and cozy and inviting, the way her neighbor, Mrs. Baldino's, house felt.

She smiled sadly at Satter, "I guess four walls don't always make a home." She laughed, shaking her melancholy away. "Well, I hope you stick around town for a while." She glanced shyly at the boy. "Will you?"

"Don't know yet, Rose. If I had my druthers, I'd be hopping the rails to find my pot of gold. But like I said, I have some reasons to stay. At least for the time being."

To hide her pleasure, Rose looked away. The nearby family had gathered their things, and was headed toward a parked sedan. This reminded her she still had a birthday present to buy. She brushed crumbs off her apron and stood up.

"Well, I best be getting home. It was nice meeting you, Satter. I hope you get the job at Penney's." She'd reluctantly turned to leave, when Satter stopped her.

"Will I see you again?"

"I don't, um, get out much."

"I'll be down at the café on Main this Saturday night. Come if you can."

"We'll see. Bye, now." Rose hurried away.

When she finally crawled into bed that night, Rose allowed herself to daydream about Satter. There was something about him she liked; but, she warned herself, good Italian girls didn't fall for drifters. Or shouldn't.

Chapter Two

*R*ose heard a clap of thunder as she replaced the kettle's lid.

Good, the garden could use some rain.

Taking a satisfied sniff, she enjoyed the aroma of tomatoes, garlic, onions, and oregano that had simmered for hours on the coal stove. Cooking had made the house unbearably hot, but it was worth the discomfort to please Papa.

In honor of his birthday, Rose had splurged on some yellow daisies from House of Flowers. Their brightness made the plank table, covered with oilcloth, more festive. She arranged the napkins the special way Sister Mary Bernadine had showed her and set two places. Stepping back, she admired the overall affect.

Unable to resist, she pulled out Papa's present, carefully wrapped in newspaper and string, from under the table. She'd spent all afternoon the day before looking for the perfect gift. Finally, she'd found a pair of suspenders — dark leather with brass fasteners — that met her approval. It had cost half her secret money, so she hoped they met Papa's approval, too.

Looking at the clock, she saw it was ten minutes after seven o'clock.

Every day except Friday, her father trod the footbridge towards home, covered in coal dust from working at the railroad round-house. On Fridays, which were paydays, he always came home late in the night. He spent a good portion of his paycheck at the bars, so when he finally did come home, he was drunk and banging into things. Most times he'd make his clumsy way to his bedroom, but sometimes Rose found him on the kitchen floor collapsed in his own vomit.

Even when she had to clean up after her father, she preferred him drunk to sober. When he was sober, she had to be very careful. Papa's moods were unpredictable, and when he was in a bad one, Rose paid the price.

The windows shook, as another thunderclap boomed overhead. An eerie dusk descended. Rose hoped Papa wouldn't get drenched on his way home. That would surely put him in a bad mood.

Finally hearing her father's step, Rose felt her stomach tighten momentarily, and then she looked at the pretty table. *Tonight will be different. Papa will like what I've done.* She quickly smoothed her apron and put a smile on her face.

Her father scowled when he saw her, slamming the door behind him.

"What's this?" he growled, throwing his soiled work gloves on the table, crushing a folded napkin.

Sante Gino Padroni clung to his thick accent, which irked Rose to no end. She felt that if one lived in Beloved America, one should talk like an American. Still, she'd never had the courage to express her feelings to her father.

"Happy birthday, Papa."

"Humph." His shoulders sagged as he pumped cold water over his blackened hands. Inky soap bubbles laced the sink's surface when he'd finished. His back was rigid as he dried his hands on a clean cloth, hanging by a nail.

Rose watched mutely. A feeling of dread budded in her abdomen. "I made your favorite meal, Papa." She removed the dirty gloves, dished pasta and sauce onto his plate, and placed it in front of him.

"Mr. Stranges sent his best wishes for you, Papa. He gave us a loaf of his wife's delicious bread for a present. Wasn't that thoughtful?" That was only partly true. He had really given the loaf to Rose, but she hoped the Lord forgave the white lie.

"Humph." He pushed the basket of bread away. "I don't need nothing from no greasy, rich *dago!*"

"Papa, he's one of our own!"

"Watch your mouth, girl." He looked at the table, then accusingly at her. "The vino?"

Rose hurried to the counter and poured from the bottle a glass of Papa's homemade wine. Ironically, it was called Dago Red. The cellar was stacked with many such bottles. Papa refused to join the neighborhood in pig butchering or tending a big garden or growing rose bushes, but he never forsook making his wine.

With a grunt, he began stuffing food into his mouth. Rose silently crossed herself to bless the meal, and watched him for any positive reaction.

"Father Nick sends his regards, too, Papa." She spoke brightly. "He says there's a summer party at the church this Sunday, and you should come!"

"And does he expect me to tell my boss I can't work because of a party at church?" Papa spat the words out. "Unlike your precious Father Nick, I have to *earn* my wages. No big church feeds and shelters me!" He threw his napkin down and pushed his plate away. It clinked into his wineglass, spilling a red drop onto the oilcloth.

Rose tasted bile, but quickly reached beneath the table. "Papa, I bought you a birthday present! They were on special at Woolworth's," she said, holding the box out to him. She forced her hand to be steady, as he grabbed it.

He tore the wrapping off and tossed it to the floor. He stared at the suspenders for a moment, then at Rose. His face contorted as he swept the remnants of dinner crashing to the floor.

"I don't need charity from no one, *especially you, girl.*" He folded the suspenders in half and stood up.

"Papa, it's a *present,* not charity!" Rose wailed, suddenly realizing her danger. She put up her arms in useless protection.

Pain seared across her shoulders, as he struck her. Shrieking, she scrambled under the table and curled into a tight ball. Covering her head with her hands, she trembled, not knowing when the next blow would come. Expecting it, though. She held her breath, as the clock stopped its ticking.

For the longest moment, the world was muffled in a quiet lull — a false serenity that Rose knew better than to trust. When the brass suspenders hit the floor close to her face, she screamed and scrunched tighter. The back door slammed. Was it over? *So soon?* Before opening her eyes, she waited. And waited. Finally, releasing a tremulous stream of air, Rose slowly crawled from under the table. She swallowed painfully, as racking sobs threatened to break her ribs.

Thunder rumbled in the distance, as she bent down and picked up pieces of broken crockery and twisted daisies.

Rose stopped talking. Nick had ceased shoveling as soon as he heard the emotion in her voice. He reached for her hand.

"You look so much like him, Nicky."

Rose paced from one end of the house to the other. Seven, eight, nine . . . When she reached ten, she'd whirl around and storm off in the opposite direction. Soon the walls closed in, and she felt claustrophobic. Flinging the front door open, she fled into the wet, turbulent twilight.

Lightening whipped across the sky, temporarily illuminating the alley where she stood. Somehow, she'd wandered into Shantytown. Dimly lit windows stared from the faces of the buildings, daring the wayward wanderer to enter their world.

"Hey, kid! Whatcha doing out in this weather?"

Rose saw a woman standing in a shadowed recess of the nearest bungalow. A cigarette flared red for a second. In the glow, she could see the woman beckoning her.

Rose turned to go, knowing she shouldn't speak to such a person, but the thought of Papa stopped her. *Why go home? Nothing was there but misery!*

"Come here and get warm, you hear?"

The woman's voice sounded vaguely familiar. Though Rose felt her Catholic conscience tugging like a cranky child, she hesitated.

The cigarette arced into the air, and was quickly extinguished by a rain puddle. "You coming, kid?" The screen door squeaked, and Rose saw the woman waiting for her.

Subduing a shiver, she dashed across the alley.

The room was small, with a neatly made bed against the wall. A dresser that had seen better days stood beside it, a pitcher and washbowl on top. They shared space with an oil lamp, the room's only source of light. A framed photograph of a smiling, tousle-haired boy leaned against the lamp.

Rose noticed several dresses hanging from a hook on the wall. Near the dresses, a small mirror was placed at eye level. Below the mirror was the only chair, a flowered apron thrown across its wooden seat.

"Make yourself comfortable, kid." The woman watched her with amused eyes.

Studiously avoiding the bed, she headed for the chair.

"Hey, better not sit on that; it's a bit unsteady." The woman handed a cotton robe to Rose. "The bed don't bite."

The robe enveloped her in warmth and the scent of lavender water. Ignoring the sting across her shoulders, she gingerly sat on the edge of the bed, and looked at the woman.

Rose was surprised. Unlike the other prostitutes she'd seen, this one wore little makeup, just a touch of scarlet lipstick. The woman's complexion was like ivory, and her dark hair was parted on the side, hugging her scalp in ironed waves. Friendliness softened her wide mouth, and Rose responded to her smile. Her summer dress hung nicely on her tall, big-boned figure, its color complementing her light eyes. Her voice was husky as she introduced herself.

"Name's Mari, with an 'i'. You look like one of them Eye-talians. Lots of them around here, I noticed."

"M-my name is Rose. Like the flower." She pointed vaguely in the direction of Little Italy. "I live a little ways from here."

Rose stifled a giggle, as the woman's hip bumped the dresser, sending the picture of the boy crashing to the floor. *For goodness sake, the woman was a Clydesdale.*

"Ouch! Damn, this place is so small, a cockroach would feel crowded." She laughed heartily at her own joke as she stooped to retrieve the picture. Kissing her finger, she pressed it to the boy's features before replacing it on the dresser.

"Sorry, kid, didn't mean to cuss in front of you. I forget in front of Teddy, too. That's my boy." She tapped the picture.

"You have a child?" Rose glanced around the room.

"Oh, he don't live with me; he lives with my pa and ma. This ain't no place for him. Course, Pa's meaner than a damn — I mean, he's not real nice, but my brothers and sisters keep Teddy out of the old man's way. I get to see him on Saturdays, when I'm not working."

Mari's mention of her "work" reminded Rose that good Italian girls didn't converse with the likes of this woman, nice as she was.

"I really should go, ma'am. My father . . . "

"Oh sure, kid, I know how a pa can be. Are you warm, yet?"

Rose realized she felt much better. She slipped out of the robe and handed it to the woman. "I'm ever grateful, ma'am."

"Call me Mari, why don't you?'

"Thank you," Rose said from the doorway. "Mari."

The next morning, Rose woke up with the dawn, as usual. She thought of Mari first thing. Her kindness had been as welcome as rainfall in a drought, and had strangely given Rose the courage to go home. The woman didn't act anything like what she'd thought a bawdy woman would.

Another thought crowded in.

What would Father Nick say if he knew I've been to Shantytown? And Papa? Rose's hands flew to her cheeks. As disappointed as Father Nick would be, her father would likely kill her if he ever found out! There was only one thing to do — she must vow never to go there again. Not even to see Mari.

Hoping twelve *Our Fathers* would cover her sins, she stoked the coal embers in the stove while she recited them. Enough heat was generated to boil water for Papa's coffee. She knocked softly on his bedroom door before entering. He almost never answered her knock. She found him as she usually did — snoring and entangled in bedcovers like he'd fought demons all night.

His face was vulnerable in sleep, and Rose could see why Mama might have loved him. In slumber, hints of strength and character could be seen in his craggy lines. She was sure he'd been handsome before loss, bitterness, and drink had maimed his countenance. He just looked old now.

"Papa, it's time to get up," she whispered in his ear. She left the steaming cup on the makeshift nightstand, a wooden crate. The only evidence that he ever heard her was, when she came home in the afternoon, the empty cup was always on the table.

Rose picked up the chamber pot and left, clicking the door shut behind her.

The morning was already warm and muggy. The rare humidity caused by last night's storm stole Rose's breath, as she stepped outside. Mrs. Baldino, her nearest neighbor, leaned against the adjoining picket fence, tossing feed on the ground. Chickens dashed furiously around her feet.

"Oh, Rose," she cooed. "I have something for you."

Rose loved the woman, whose apple-cheeked face was often creased into a large smile. She was as sweet as her *torrone*, a delicious nougat made of honey, sugar, hazelnuts, and egg whites. At Christmastime, Mrs. Baldino gave a basket of the special treat to everyone, but her thoughtfulness wasn't limited to just the holiday season or to confections. She was the closest thing Rose had to a mother.

Mrs. Baldino's friendship was Rose's mainstay, especially since Papa had disrespected Mr. Alonzi, Little Italy's *compare* and benefactor. Mr. Alonzi had told Papa he needed to be a better provider and father, to which Papa had told him to "go to hell." Since Papa refused to apologize, the Italian community, which thrived on goodwill, had no choice but to alienate him. Alienation generally brought a speedy apology — and balance — back to the community. So far, it hadn't worked on Papa.

"How do, Ma'am. I'm on my way to the church. Can I pick something up from the grocery this afternoon? Some olives, maybe?"

"Our pantry's full, dear one. I thought you could use another length of salami and some canned apricots."

Rose sniffed the spiciness of the cured meat. The yearly pig butchering yielded a harvest that filled shelves and larders: sausage, bacon, salami, and ham came from the meat; leftovers made headcheese, cracklings and soap. Rose joined Mrs. Baldino's family when they butchered, and shared some of the bounty.

"Thank you very much, ma'am." Rose arranged the salami and the jars of amber fruit carefully in her arms. "Papa thanks you, too."

"All of Little Italy could smell your spaghetti sauce, yesterday. I hope your papa liked it." She tilted her head, eyes round with concern.

Rose rotated her aching shoulder, and said, "Papa liked it fine. Thank you for asking, ma'am. I should go now."

Mrs. Baldino pressed Rose's hand. "You don't have to take it."

"Oh, we could use the provisions."

"That's not what I mean."

Rose looked at the ground, embarrassed with sudden understanding. "What choice do I have?"

Turning, she walked back to the house and deposited Mrs. Baldino's gifts on the counter. Hearing her father moving in his room, she left quickly.

Mrs. Baldino is right. This is no way to live. Maybe Father Nick can tell me what to do.

Chapter Three

*"**G**ive that to me, Nicky. I'll keep it — to remember." Nick handed his grandmother the baseball-sized concrete marker he'd dug up. She brushed at the dirt.*

"Such an insignificant way to commemorate someone's life, Nicky."

St. Joe's was like a second home to Rose. It was warm and welcoming and beautiful. She loved the tower that extended many feet above the brick building, holding aloft the holy cross. The wooden entrance doors opened to the sanctuary lined on both sides with stained glass windows. Rows of oak pews led up to the magnificent altar, and above the entrance of the church was a spacious choir loft.

The pastor of St. Joe's, Father Nicholas Bertrand, was a persuasive man, whose sermons were known to turn many a soul toward saintliness. He also played the pipe organ, and spent many hours with the choir. Father Nick, a native of Luxembourg, had many passions besides God and music. While active as a speaker and a promoter of goodwill in the city, his greatest love was children. He was very concerned about their education and welfare.

St. Joe's had a parochial school, and Father Nick visited its classrooms regularly. The schoolchildren adored him. Rose envied the students, since Papa forbid her to attend the school. Still, she consoled herself, Grand Junction High School had excellent teachers, and she'd made a couple of good friends there.

Whenever Rose entered the sanctuary, she was stirred by her surroundings. A different sensation greeted her each time she walked through the double doors. Some days she drank in the clean smell of lemon oil on seasoned wooden pews. Other times she wondered at the beautiful altar, its dark butternut imbued with unapproachable mystery. There were profound moments when Rose felt woven into the quiet atmosphere of richly colored history, somber faith, and comforting ritual. Watching from the walls, the stained glass saints seemed to encourage her that she wasn't alone on life's journey.

Members of St. Joe's had donated the windows. Each was arched and framed in uniform pieces of colored glass, with the name of the benefactors etched in banners along the bottoms.

Rose loved these windows. Her favorite depiction was the one where a crimson heart was wreathed by a chain of roses and set against a deep blue background. At the crown of the window was a descending dove.

It was here she found Father Nick. He was in coveralls and work boots, cleaning the window. Tufts of silver hair bushed out in the humidity, and sweat dribbled down his forehead. He stood on a ladder that angled from the cream walls, a cloth and pail perched on a rung at his elbow. Several more pails of water and piles of clean cloths were assembled on the floor.

"Father, may I speak with you? It's important."

"Of course, my girl! I'm always at your disposal." The priest's blue-green eyes crinkled when he smiled.

Rose thought they were nice eyes.

He began to descend the ladder.

"Don't come down, Father. Please continue your work and I'll help you while we talk." Having something to do with her hands would make it easier to tell him about Papa.

"Aren't you the industrious one? Well, I could use an extra pair of hands." The priest mopped his face with a handkerchief. "After I soap the window, I'll need clean cloths for rinsing. Wring them almost dry, my girl. These windows need special care."

Rose fell into a rhythm of bending, dipping, wringing, and exchanging clean cloth for dirty. "I love this window especially, Father."

He leaned back and looked at it. "It is captivating. What do you think it symbolizes?"

Rose gazed upward. "The dove is the Holy Spirit, and I'm pretty sure the heart is Jesus. The roses . . . hmm. Perhaps they are the people who draw near to our Lord and love Him." She tilted her head in thought. "Do you think our love smells as sweet to Jesus, as a rose does to us?"

"I'm sure it is a lovely fragrance to Him, indeed." Father Nick climbed down the ladder, and rested against a pew. He motioned for Rose to join him. "I see something amazing when I look at a stained glass window. Would you like to know what it is?"

Rose nodded, eagerly.

"I see a perfectly crafted masterpiece of beauty and message. The amazing thing is, if the artist had left out even one bit of glass, the picture would be incomplete. No matter how small or colorless, each piece is necessary and valuable."

Rose knitted her eyebrows in bewilderment. "And why is that amazing, Father?"

"Because it is the way our Creator views His favorite creation. Humanity. To Him, we are His most magnificent masterpiece. No matter what size, shape, color, or character, God loves and values us equally.

"Unfortunately, *we* don't always value each other, as God does. That's why hatred, bigotry, prejudice and avarice are prevalent in this world." The priest sighed.

"If only we saw through God's eyes, Rose. Then the light of His love would be illuminated through us," Father Nick swept his hand to include the wall of sparkling windows, "just as the sun illuminates these. What a beautiful world we'd live in, if that happened more often."

Rose was silent for a long moment. Ignoring the tightness in her throat, she asked, "How does the Lord see those who hurt others, Father?"

"Christ loved even those who crucified Him." The priest paused, and looked down at the girl. "Rose, has someone hurt you?"

Reluctantly, she moved the collar of her dress to reveal her bruised shoulder. "Papa has," she whispered.

"Dear girl!"

Before she knew it, Rose was wrapped in Father Nick's compassionate arms. She felt warm and protected, as if God Himself was embracing her. Relaxing into that comfort, she buried her face in the priest's shoulder and wept.

"Are you sure you won't stay tonight with the sisters?" Father Nick and Rose stood outside the entrance of the sanctuary. Rose shielded her eyes from the sun.

"He won't come home until late tonight, Father. It's payday." She handed the priest his handkerchief.

"How are you feeling, now?"

"Our talk helped more than you know. Thank you."

Father Nick's face became serious. "Rose, don't let him strike you again. The church will offer sanctuary whenever you need it."

Rose nodded, then stood on tiptoe and kissed the priest's cheek. "Thank you. I guess I better get to the office. Sister Mary Bernadine mentioned school desks that need cleaning."

"Hey, kid! Nice to see you again."

Rose had been walking down Main Street, deep in thought. She was jolted out of her reverie by the one person she had hoped to avoid forever.

In front of the beauty shop, Mari was helping an elderly woman from the passenger side of a dark car. After propping her against the fender, Mari folded the front seat down. From the inner recesses, she struggled to pull out a wheelchair.

While she's busy, I'll make a quick escape, Rose thought. Then she remembered her conversation with Father Nick. He'd said no matter what size, shape, color or character, God loved all people. *Does that include prostitutes, Father?* Rose considered this question and then nodded, feeling sure the priest would say that even people like Mari were included. Happiness filled Rose. Perhaps she could keep her new friend, after all.

"Here, let me lend a hand."

As she helped Mari, Rose tried not to stare at the curious old woman. Plumes of silver lace cascaded from her bodice, elbows and hem. Her feathered hat was tilted, shading one large, moist eye. Rose choked on the heavy scent of Larkspur lotion that eddied around her. The woman grinned, revealing numerous gaps and — could it be — the glint of a diamond embedded in one front tooth.

"It's like trying to deliver a breech calf!" Mari guffawed. With a jarring clatter, she and Rose finally deposited the wheelchair on the street.

"You'd think they'd make these things to collapse." She moved the chair beside the fender. "Here you go, Emma. Have a seat."

Mari plopped the old woman unceremoniously into the wheelchair. Rose giggled, as the clearly irritated woman adjusted her hat. From the recesses of her frilly bosom, the woman pulled out a lacy handkerchief and dabbed at her face.

It was then Rose saw her clubfoot.

"Iris, meet Emma Splott, my boss."

"It's Rose. My name is *Rose*, madam; Er, that is, *ma'am*." The girl felt her cheeks grow hot. "How do you do?"

Emma extended her hand, palm down, as if expecting it to be kissed. Age spots landscaped the woman's wrinkled skin, but her nails were manicured and painted bright pink. Her grasp was surprisingly strong.

"Oops, sorry kid. I knew it was a flower of some kind." Mari looked embarrassed as she twirled the wheelchair toward the storefronts.

"Never mind, *girl!*"

Emma's words were splashy and had a slight foreign sound to them. Rose couldn't place her accent.

Turning her attention to Rose, the old woman rearranged her scowl into a tense smile.

"My, you are pretty," she said smoothly. "If we had time, we'd love to visit with you, but we are late for an appointment." Emma shot Mari a stabbing look. "So, let us proceed, shall we?"

As she pushed Emma past Rose, Mari whispered for her to wait, she'd be back in a minute.

Rose stepped into the shade of the doorway, fanning herself with her hand. Two doors down, the group of beautiful ladies that Rose had encountered a few days earlier, strolled out of Fashion Tailors. They turned toward Rose, arms full of purchases.

Looking down at her threadbare dress, she suddenly was self-conscious. *One day I'll dress pretty, too.*

"Hello, again." Darla was lovelier than Rose remembered. The woman nodded regally at Rose, as the group passed her.

Rose felt like curtseying.

She was still watching them saunter down the sidewalk, when Mari emerged from the beauty shop.

"Her Majesty will be busy for a few hours now. Takes a long time to get that tornado of hair tidy again." She snorted. "Hey, kid," Mari tapped Rose's shoulder. "You know them there women?"

Rose shook her head, her eyes still on the ladies' gently swaying figures. "No, but I wish I did. They're lovely."

"Hmm. Hey, I got some time to kill; what say we go have a malted? We can take my car." Mari patted the hood. "A beauty, ain't it? Thirty-six Packard Touring Coup-ay." She opened her door, and looked at Rose standing on the sidewalk. "You coming?"

Rose faltered. What if someone saw her with Mari? What if Papa saw? Pain sliced her shoulder where her father had struck her, and she shivered in spite of the hot, muggy day. This caused anger to surge through her. *Who cares what Papa thinks?* A malted sounded real good.

Rose tossed her braid over her shoulder and stepped onto the street, pulling open the passenger door.

She felt a thrill, as the car traveled down Main Street. "I've only ridden in one other car — my friend Marj's — but Agony's not nearly as nice as this."

"Got it in my divorce settlement. Glad something good came from being hitched to that weak-minded titty baby." Mari drove into a parking space, and pulled the brake. Her voice softened. "Course, I got Teddy. He's a titty baby, too, but I love him."

"Didn't you love your husband?"

"Once."

Rose saw the set of Mari's mouth, and refrained from further questions.

"Here we are, kid. Good ol' Hotel D'Hamburger. Got a boyfriend that washes dishes here."

Before she could stop herself, Rose asked, "Are you allowed to have boyfriends? I mean, in your profession . . ." Her voice dwindled.

"What do you mean, 'my profession'?" Mari looked at Rose for a second, and then burst into loud guffaws. "You think I'm a — !" Another stanza of staccato laughter. Mari covered her face with her hands, and the whole car shook with her mirth.

By this time, Rose was thoroughly confused. The woman seemed demented.

Tears were streaming down Mari's cheeks when she finally looked at Rose again. "Woo, kid, I haven't laughed that hard in years!"

Rose ventured a smile. "You're not a — a prostitute?"

Mari wiped her eyes with the back of hand. Little giggles still escaped. "I can see where you mighta gotten the idea, sure enough. No kid, I ain't no bawdy woman. Anyone ask me to bed a fella for money, I'll knock him flat.

"See, I'm just the housekeeper and driver for Her Majesty. You mighta noticed she's a cripple. I answered her advertisement 'bout a week ago. Oh!" Mari turned her head, her eyes wide. Another burst of laughter echoed around the interior of the car.

"You poor baby! Them high-class ladies you was drooling over a minute ago? *They're* the prostitutes!"

"You can stop your hooting and hollering, young man. Remember where you are." Rose tapped Nick's shoulder with the flashlight.

Nick's laughter squelched into a hiccup, as he indeed remembered where he was. After making sure he hadn't roused the dead, he smiled at his grandmother. "Nonna, I would have thought it easy to tell a lady of the evening from a, you know, decent woman."

"Uffa, see what you know! Like Darla, some wore the latest fashions and conducted themselves like ladies — at least in public. They didn't generally talk to anyone they met on the streets for fear of embarrassing a prominent businessman or two. And they weren't supposed to speak to young girls, because it would have been thought they were enlisting."

"But, Darla — "

"I don't know why Darla spoke to me, but her attentions had been flattering. On the other hand, Emma Splott scared me. I still remember those liquid eyes trolling the depths of my soul, like she hoped to hook something as slippery as she."

The interior of the diner was cool. The Hotel D'Hamburger was one of the few places in the city where air conditioning was installed. The smell of grilled hamburgers and French-fried potatoes filled the air. A counter stood at the back near the kitchen door. The Wurlitzer jukebox was playing a song, its bubbles dancing in the changing blues, reds, greens, and yellows of the neon tubes.

"Oh, I love this tune!" Mari started wagging a finger in the air and swinging her hips as she headed for the nearest booth.

Rose sidled into the opposite seat, as Mari started singing loudly.

"The moon in all its splendor, your kiss so very tender, the words when you surrender, to meeeee."

By this time the waitress had come over and joined Mari, their cheeks together as they sang. Just then, Mari hopped up and began dancing with the waitress. Astonished, Rose watched Mari slide the woman between her legs. The waitress popped up behind her, grabbed Mari's outstretched hand and twirled around.

Embarrassed by the attention the two were drawing, Rose sunk deeper in her seat.

When the song had ended, Mari fell into the booth with a sigh. "Olive Blackburn, you cut a swell rug!"

"And you're a knocked-out alligator!" Olive's breathless voice boomed over Rose's head. "Whew," she wiped her upper lip. "Now, what can I get you gals?"

Mari shooed the menu away.

"Olive makes the best malteds in town. What flavor do you want, kid? Chocolate, strawberry, or vanilla?"

They both agreed on chocolate, and Olive sashayed away, humming and waving a finger in the air.

On the table was a music box that took nickels for songs. Mari flipped the selections back and forth until she found one she liked, and inserted a coin.

"Tommy Dorsey is my favorite band. That last tune, *Marie,* came out in January, and *Song of India* is on the same platter. The bands at the Copeco play his songs all the time 'cause they're good jivin'."

The music was catchy, and Rose started moving her head in time to the beat. Soon she was laughing and enjoying herself.

By the time they'd slurped the last of their drinks, Rose felt more comfortable with Mari than anyone she'd ever known. There was no pretense with the woman. She may have been coarse by some folks' standards, but Rose thought her bluntness liberating. She found the young woman easy to talk with, and before she knew it, had told about her father's disastrous birthday supper.

"You should've knocked him flat, kid! Nobody should do that to you. It makes me mad when I hear of folks hitting their kin. Heck, my own pa was guilty of that. He beat all the kids, except yours truly." Mari tapped her chest. "When I was five, he raised his hand to me, but I wasn't gonna let him bruise me, like the rest. No siree! I bunched up my little fists and slugged his knees with everything I had. It never occurred to me, he could knock me silly. But, instead of giving me a walloping, he laughed and hoisted me onto his shoulder."

Rose tried to picture bunching up her fists and walloping her own Papa. She shuddered at the punishment she would surely get.

"I can remember spending a lot of time with Pa from then on. He would say I weren't no titty baby, and I would bust with pride. Most every day we tended the fields together. He even let me drive the tractor.

"When I was sixteen, the black blizzards hit the Midwest." Mari's eyes lost focus, remembering another time. "They hit Oklahoma like rolling black smoke. We had to keep the lights on all day and stuff every crack in the house with cloth. Still, dust got into everything." Mari shook her head as if to clear the unwanted memories. "Little farms were buried and towns were blackened

beyond recognition. My folks headed out here in hopes of finding work. I stayed behind and got hitched. Had Teddy that year."

Olive came over and asked if there was anything else the two
needed.

"Well, could you send that no-good Johnny out for a sec?"

"You know I'm not supposed to do that, Mari."

"Aw come on, Olive, I'll only take a minute of his time. We
need to set up a date, is all."

"You owe me, gal." The waitress put two fingers in her mouth
and let out a shrill whistle. "Hey, Johnny, get your arse out here,
will you?"

Rose's ears were still ringing, when a tall fellow squeezed into
the booth next to Mari. After a quick kiss on her cheek, he looked
over at Rose.

"Who's your little whos'it?"

"New friend. Rose meet Johnny."

His smile seemed to light up his whole face, but what caught
Rose's attention were his ears, which flanked his head like floppy
bookends. He held out his hand and enveloped Rose's in a
clammy grasp. She returned his smile, wiping her hand on her
dress under the table.

"Say, where we going tomorrow night?" Mari leaned against
Johnny's shoulder and fluttered her eyelashes. "I hear Armand de
Beque is playing all weekend at the Copeco. How 'bout we cut
the rug with his band?"

"You know I got to work until nine on Saturday evenings."

Fascinated, Rose watched Johnny's ears bob back and forth
with each word.

"That's okay. Copeco stays open late. I'll pick you up at nine
sharp."

After Johnny left, Mari muttered "titty baby" under her breath.
Rose hid a smile.

"Well, I guess I should pick up Her Majesty. Can I drop you
somewhere, kid?"

"No thanks, I can walk. Home's only a few blocks away. Say,
Mari? Was that a diamond in Emma's tooth?"

"Yup. She admired Miss Diamond Tooth Lil, who died last
year 'bout this time. Lil worked the dance halls in Alaska forty

years ago, and had quite a following, it seems." Mari grinned. "Unfortunately, by the time she died, all the friends were gone and her precious diamonds had been swallowed or lost, leaving great big holes in her teeth. "Something for our Emma to look forward to, eh?"

Chapter Four

*P*apa's snores could be heard through Rose's bedroom door. The girl stretched slowly, languishing in the warmth of the sunshine pouring from the window above her bed. Suddenly realizing the lateness of the morning, she sat up and was blinded by sunlight. Rubbing her eyes, she ran into the kitchen in her nightgown. She quickly made a cup of coffee, using last night's water from the kettle. Some of the tepid brew spilled on her hand, as she knocked on her father's door.

"Papa! Quickly, it is time to get up! Papa, please, you must wake up. You're late." A sour smell emanated from her father's skin, and Rose wrinkled her nose as she shook his shoulder with growing concern.

"What's going on here?" Papa rolled over, his features sluggish with sleep and hangover.

"I'm sorry, Papa. I slept past dawn, and now you're late. Please, you must hurry."

"You worthless girl!" he snarled, struggling to untangle his legs from his bedcovers. "Get out! I will deal with you when I get home!"

The anger on Papa's face sent Rose scurrying into the kitchen. By the time he appeared, dressed but unshaven, she had his noon meal made and wrapped. Grabbing the bundle from her hand, he slammed the door without a backward look.

She leaned against the table, shaken.

Rose didn't work at the church on Saturdays. On these days, she scoured the house. Adrenaline helped her perform her chores, and the day went quickly. After cleaning, she weeded the garden, harvesting tomatoes and lettuce to go with an antipasto salad. She sliced some of Mrs. Baldino's salami paper-thin and cubed provolone. Crushing a clove of garlic, she rubbed the inside of a wooden bowl, then tossed the ripped lettuce and diced tomatoes in to soak up the flavor. She placed all the ingredients, along with the vinaigrette she'd made, in the icebox to await suppertime.

Rose made a mental note to stop by Strange's Grocery for a tin of sardines and a loaf of bread for *crostini,* crisp bread rounds. These would complete the meal.

She hoped Papa's anger would be worked off by the time he got home. She was running out of ways to calm her father down. After his birthday, she knew even a good meal might not soothe his temper anymore.

Why can't he get himself up, anyway? I have enough to do as it is!

Rose stiffened, alarmed at her unbidden thoughts. For most of her life, she'd been happy to do whatever pleased Papa, even when he showed no appreciation for her efforts. Mrs. Baldino had told her many years ago that good Italian girls who took care of their papas, grew up to be good Italian wives. And she wanted to be a good wife. So, where had this new contrariness come from? Perhaps Mari's independent spirit was rubbing off on her.

In that case, I should put an end to our friendship. Family is the most important part of Little Italy.

But the thought of not seeing Mari again caused Rose's heart to sink. Yesterday, they'd had fun together. Fun was something she rarely experienced because life with Papa was harsh. No, she decided, I won't give up Mari, not even for Papa.

And he really should get up himself!

These last thoughts, spoken out loud, had a satisfactory sound to them. Rose whipped off her apron, and placed some coins in her skirt pocket before leaving for the grocer's.

As usual, Rose had to settle her stomach as Papa's return approached. She tweaked the kitchen curtain until it hung properly. The kitchen was pristine now. Glancing through the bedroom doorways, she nodded. Both beds were made with clean sheets and square corners. The floors were swept and burnished under the waning sunlight.

The table was set with the antipasto artfully arranged next to the salad. Rose uncorked the wine and placed it next to Papa's glass. The *crostini* lay wrapped in a cloth. She sat down to wait.

An hour later, Rose looked across to Papa's empty chair. She stood and put the cork in the untouched wine, wrapped the *crostini* in extra cloth, put the antipasto into the icebox. Then she shrugged into a sweater and went out into the deepening dusk.

Rose walked down Main Street looking for something to do. Part of her worried that she would run into Papa, and another part worried that she wouldn't. Where could he be? *Is he all right?*

Moslander's Pool Hall had an array of young men hanging out by the pool tables. Their fathers and uncles and older brothers smoked cigars and swapped stories over a glass of tap beer in the adjoining room. At school, Rose had overheard the schoolboys talk in hushed tones about the day they'd be allowed to smoke with the men. She thought it a silly initiation into manhood, but who could understand the mind of the male?

Peeking in, she saw Ivan, the football player, cue up before slamming the white ball into a triangle of colored balls. He looked proud of the results, and after spotting Rose, saluted her with a cocky grin.

"I'm feeling like a million, Rose. Wanna come in and watch me massacre these boys?" Ivan beckoned to the elevated stools for spectators.

Rose knew only males were allowed in the pool hall, so she rolled her eyes at him.

Laughter broke out. "Hey, Ivan, did the love bug bite you?"

Rose felt her face flush. She heard, "Swell girl!" before slipping into the cool evening again.

"Fiddle dee dee," she said, with a small smile.

Rose passed several movie houses with long lines of chattering people. She neared the Mission Theater. A queue of mostly Italian and Mexican families waited to pay their fare. The theater, which always featured a western, was nicknamed "the cootie exchange," which highly offended its clientele. In spite of the immigrants' many contributions to the valley over the decades, prejudice toward the newcomers had diminished only a little.

Rose loved westerns. They appealed to her sense of justice because the good guy always won. Scanning the line, she looked for any familiar face to join.

A young man wearing a worn hat reminded Rose of Satter Simpson and his invitation to meet him. She felt a spark of excitement, and the thought of a movie was forgotten.

Didn't he say he would be at the café on Main this evening? But which one?

Seven eating establishments dotted as many streets that made up downtown. Feeling a bit foolish, Rose stopped at each one, looking for Satter. After poking her head in the door of the Silver Moon Café, she wondered if she should just go home. It was nearing nine o'clock, and Satter probably had eaten his supper and moved on.

She also worried about Papa. If he hadn't gone home after work, where else might he have gone?

"Ain't you pretty as a picture!"

Surprised, Rose twirled around into the arms of Satter Simpson. He smelled of pine soap and brilliantine and freshness. Being as close as she was, she couldn't help but notice the swelling of his nose had gone down. *He's even more handsome,* she realized.

Rose quickly escaped the boy's embrace, and smoothed her skirt. Her heart pounded in her throat.

"I been waiting around for you, hoping you'd show."

All Rose could do was nod.

The boy looked up at the stars, then down at the girl.

"Nice night."

"Mmm."

His expression seemed to expect something more from her — and Rose would have liked to accommodate him — but for the life of her, she couldn't make her lips move.

"Care for supper?"

Rose nodded once more, and Satter took her by the elbow, guiding her into the light of the Silver Moon.

The café murmured with low conversation punctuated by spurts of laughter and the sizzle of grilling meat.

Rose suddenly felt ravenous.

She was momentarily alarmed when Satter seated himself next to her, rather than across the booth. If Mrs. Baldino had been there, she'd have boxed the boy's ears — and had some choice words for Rose, as well. But sitting close to Satter was intoxicating, so she silenced the woman and cast a shy glance her companion's way.

After they ordered, Rose relaxed. Satter kept up the conversation by recounting some of his adventures working odd jobs. Like a snapshot, Rose saw what a day was like for many a wandering man. Fueled by hunger and necessity, Satter's experiences had often been exciting and, sometimes, dangerous. Rose was impressed by the matter-of-factness in the young man's voice.

"It seems those hardships have made you stronger and wiser."

Satter shrugged, philosophically. "'We are face to face with our destiny, and we must meet it with a high and resolute courage.' Teddy Roosevelt."

Rose shook her head, ruefully. "Too bad the rest of the world doesn't carry his philosophy." She closed her eyes in concentration. *Now how did that poem go? Yes, that's it.* Opening her eyes, she brushed at her bangs and recited:

"Troubled, worried days, these,
Full of wars, unhappiness, deceit;
And men who sneak, and lie, and cheat,
For that is ease."

Rose answered the question in Satter's eyes. "Hazlett Wubben. A friend from school."

"Ah. These are decaying times, that's for sure, Rose. The future is filled with frightening possibilities, and if something ain't done soon, the world will go to hell in a hand basket."

"You shouldn't be so cynical, Satter. Listen how Hazlett's poem ends:

"We must contain some good part,
Conscious of beauty, love, life;

Cannot peacefulness conquer strife,
And triumphant reign the heart?"

Rose squeezed the boy's hand. "That's the only way this dreary old world can be redeemed, Satter. By holding on to what is good."

At that moment, the waitress slid Rose's hamburger and French-fried potatoes in front of her. She dug in with relish. Satter's steak continued to sizzle, while he sliced off a large piece and stuffed it into his mouth. He chewed around his words.

"Sounds reasonable if good didn't look so much like evil these days. Nothing is what it seems." Satter pointed his fork across the room. "See that fella over there?"

Rose saw an older man who looked the picture of a Southern Colonel in Civil War days. His long white hair fell neatly to his shoulders, while a droopy mustache framed fleshy lips. He wore a dark suit, crisp shirt and black bow tie. A funny little hat perched on his knee, while a cane rested against the booth. He scrutinized each bite he took, sniffing first, then touching his tongue to it, before closing his eyes and putting it in his mouth.

"He appears to be the perfect gentleman, but it wouldn't surprise me if he was crazier than a hound dog in a holler. These days, a man could just as well be your kindly granddaddy as a political enemy trying to kill you."

"But, he looks so sweet."

"Where people are concerned, Rose, you never know what's under the paint."

"What about him?"

Rose lifted her chin toward the table nearest them. A young man was reading a well-worn book, while his hamburger grew cold. She could barely make out the title, *20,000 Leagues Under the Sea*. Every few moments he would lick the tip of his pencil and make a note on the margin of a page.

"What do you think is under *his* paint?"

"Hmm." Satter rubbed his chin. "He looks like his engine's running but ain't no one driving." He flashed her a wicked grin.

The waitress interrupted the man, asking if he needed anything more. Rose heard her call him Everett. He gave her a goofy smile and shook his head before returning to the book.

Rose leaned her cheek on her hand and sighed. "No, he looks more like a dreamer; a solitary wanderer in love with beauty and searching for a peaceful world."

Satter's expression soured. "Won't find such a place! Pain and sorrow is what this world's about. Nothing but suffering here."

"Stuff and nonsense!" Rose glared at Satter. "There's much more to life than suffering. Besides, suffering refines us. Look how it's affected you. You're strong, determined and — under the paint — even hopeful. You don't fool me, Satter Simpson. When it counts, you will make sure good wins."

Satter lifted his soda and drank deeply. Wiping his mouth across the back of his sleeve, he pushed his empty glass across the table.

"I sure hope so, Rose."

In spite of her profuse objections, Satter walked Rose home. She was afraid Papa would be watching for her, and she didn't want the boy to see him upset. She thanked the good Lord when she saw the dark windows.

She was tongue-tied when it came time to say goodbye. Rose wanted the evening to go on forever. She didn't pull her hand back, when Satter reached for it in the moonlight.

"Stay as sweet as you are, Rose. We'll be seeing each other again." Satter's lips barely touched the palm of her hand, but it burned as if ignited. The shadows swallowed him, as he softly called her name.

The house had a deserted feel to it when Rose opened the door, and she exhaled when she saw Papa wasn't waiting in the dark. Humming tunelessly, she rummaged through the coals in the belly of the stove, stoking up the heat. She put on a kettle of water to use for her nighttime ritual.

After pulling her cotton nightgown over her head, she began brushing her hair.

The pearl-handled brush had belonged to her mother, as well as the matching handheld mirror. They were the only things, besides a wedding picture, that she had of her mother. Normally the sight and the feel of them brought her comfort. Tonight, she wished her mother were sitting on the bed with her, so she could talk about these new feelings roiling around in her gut.

Holding up the mirror, she examined her face closely.

Her eyes seemed different, shining with a maturity that hadn't been there the day before. Even her lips seemed fuller, more knowing in their set. It wasn't altogether disturbing — this new Rose — yet, it would take some getting used to.

She wondered how Satter saw her. Girl or woman? She sighed, remembering his touch. Would her lips have burned if they'd been kissed, too?

"Who do you see in that mirror, girl?"

Rose had not heard the door open. Stunned, she dropped the mirror, watching in horror as it tumbled to the floor. A thin crack etched its way across the glass.

"Papa!" she cried, as she scooped it up and held it against her breast. "That was Mama's!"

"Do you see a stupid girl, like I see? A worthless girl who don't know how to take care of her papa? Who brings dishonor and shame to him? That's who I see!"

The man turned, and Rose wanted to hurl the broken mirror at his retreating back. Instead, she flung herself on her pillow and burst into tears.

How long had he been watching, and had he read her thoughts? She felt ashamed and she felt rage and she felt despair. Would Papa ever love her?

Chapter Five

*T*he next week, Rose went about her business but avoided Papa as much as possible. Suppertime was the most uncomfortable, and she thought of feigning illness to avoid sitting across the table from him. Often she caught him watching her. One time his eyes seemed thoughtful, and she hoped he would apologize. It had been a vain hope, for his eyes had hardened and he'd turned and lumbered into his bedroom, closing the door behind him.

Rose wondered what she would have done if he had apologized. A week ago, it might have been the beginning of a new relationship, the kind other daughters had with their fathers. A week ago, pleasing Papa had been her whole reason for living, but that had changed. Now, there was Satter.

By Friday, not ten words had been exchanged between father and daughter. When Rose left for the church, Mrs. Baldino called out to her.

"The neighborhood has been quiet this week. Things must be going better for you, dear one."

"Yes, ma'am."

Mrs. Baldino beamed at her, while clucking chickens waddled around her ankles.

Rose smiled back.

Actually, the lack of communication suited Rose. If she and Papa weren't speaking, then she wouldn't have to tell him she was going on a date that evening with Satter. Not that he'd notice her absence, anyway. It was payday.

In the Old Country, good Italian girls didn't date. Marriages were arranged by their parents, and a girl was lucky to even meet her spouse before her wedding day. Rose secretly feared Papa would never seek a husband for her. He could keep her under his roof until his dying day, and there was no way she was going to let that happen!

Satter had gotten the job at J.C. Penney's. He worked long hours: 7:30 a.m. to 7 p.m. weekdays, and until 10 p.m. on Saturdays. He was a hard worker, and his efforts paid off quickly. Within a few days, his boss had promoted him from stock clerk to fitting shoes.

Rose stopped in every day to say hello. The young man's face always lit up when he saw her, which made Rose glow. If not waiting on a customer, Satter would pull her behind the stock-room curtain, and they'd exchange pleasantries. The emerging buds of womanhood Papa had crushed the night Mama's mirror cracked began to blossom again, and Rose's feelings for the boy grew stronger.

After saying goodbye to Mrs. Baldino, Rose decided on a quick visit to J.C. Penney's. She walked through the glass entry and searched for Satter. She didn't see his head over the aisles, nor was he helping a customer. Peeking behind the stockroom cur-tain, she saw he wasn't there, either. Finally, she asked his boss. Mr. Class seemed annoyed when he explained the boy had not come in yet. He turned away from Rose when an older man in a white hat approached.

"Good morning, Sheriff Lumley. How may I help you?"

The sheriff's voice was full of good cheer. "Mornin', Emerson." He pumped the salesman's hand while clapping him soundly on the shoulder. "Need some new shoes, son. These ol' soles are worn out," he winked at the salesman, "from all the politickin' I've been doin', lately." He clapped the man's shoulder once more. "I'm sure I can count on your vote again this election, eh?"

Mr. Class nodded vigorously. "Of course, sir. Now about those shoes . . . " The two men strolled away from Rose.

She left the department store and walked to the church, worried and praying nothing was wrong with Satter. She felt deep disap-pointment at not seeing him, and hoped their date was still on.

Sister Mary Bernadine sent Rose over to the sanctuary to pol-ish pews. The mindless repetitiveness of the task allowed Rose to mull over her feelings for Satter.

"I think the cloth works better if you put polish on it." Father Nick smiled down from the choir loft.

"Hello, Father. I didn't know anyone was here." Rose examined her cloth and discovered it was dry. She picked up the lemon oil.

"Just working on Sunday's sermon. It's quiet up here, and," he looked over his shoulder, "Sister Mary Bernadine can't find me."

He watched Rose put the polish back down on the pew without dampening her cloth.

"Is there something on your mind, Rose?" His blue-green eyes were calm, as he gazed down at her.

"Um, no Father. Everything is fine."

"How have you and your papa fared, lately?"

"Fine, Father. I hardly see him these days."

"And Sister Mary Bernadine has not been overworking you, now has she?"

"Oh, no, Father. She has been fine, too."

"Hmm. Well I'm glad to see all is — fine."

"Yes, Father."

Satter's hand was still poised to knock on the door, when Rose jerked it open. "Where have you been?"

"Picking you daisies."

His scrubbed face shone above a paisley tie, which, Rose noted, strangely complemented his checkered jacket and starched white shirt. She took the bouquet, tied by a string, that the young man presented.

"My favorite color," Rose caressed a yellow petal, then glanced at Satter. "Since I didn't see you today, I wondered if you'd show up for our date."

"Aw Rose, I'd never stand you up."

Rose stepped onto the porch and closed the door behind her. She waited for an explanation.

Satter gulped at her expression. "Truth is, my nephew came down awful sick last night. My sister asked me to drive him to Doc Munro's this morning, since she couldn't leave work. By the time I dropped the boy off, the morning was almost gone. I stopped by the store, hoping I hadn't lost my job, but Mr. Class, God bless the man, understood and let me work the rest of my shift."

Satter knew he was running off at the mouth, but Rose still didn't look convinced. He pulled at the starched collar of his shirt. "Um, then, I wanted to clean up a bit and purchase these here flowers for you."

He punched Rose's shoulder good-naturedly. "You ain't sore no more, are you?"

Rose returned Satter's punch, maybe a little harder than was necessary. "I suppose not. I better find something to put these flowers in."

She thought of asking Satter inside, but noticed Mrs. Baldino had appeared on her porch. The woman waved to Rose, but her face lacked friendliness. Rose waved back, then whispered to Satter, "Wait here."

When she stepped onto the porch again, she'd donned a sweater. The couple strolled down the walkway side-by-side, a good two feet between them. Smiling and nodding at Mrs. Baldino, Satter commented on the lovely evening. The woman's brows came together. She called out that the newspaper had predicted unsettled weather, and they'd better be careful. Behind those words, Rose heard the warning that good Italian girls did not go off alone with a boy.

"Uh, oh!"

"What is it, Rose?"

"Let me handle this," she whispered.

"Is there a problem?" Satter asked as his gaze followed hers.

Rose shushed him, and then smoothed her dress before saying, "Good evening, Mr. Alonzi."

Little Italy's most prestigious and wealthiest citizen leaned against the wall of his liquor store, smoking his evening cigar.

Amore Alonzi was an excellent businessman, but most of his wealth came from helping his *paesani* establish their families in the valley. While some had left the Old Country because of the sparse economy, many had fled in fear of the Black Hand, a terrorist group that robbed Italians of their hard-earned wealth. Highly regarded as a man of integrity, Mr. Alonzi helped families get settled and mediated between the Italian community and local businesses. If anyone had a problem, they took it to Mr. Alonzi, who found a solution. He also was godfather to many of the children born in the community, including Rose.

The stately man tipped his hat when the couple drew near. "Evening, Rose." The man's eyes slid to Satter, as he puffed on his cigar. "Where is your papa?"

"It's Friday, sir."

"Shouldn't you be at home? Perhaps Mrs. Baldino has need of you."

A smoke ring drifted by, as Rose lifted her chin. "I'm going on a date, sir."

"You know things aren't done that way around here, young lady."

Rose's heart was pounding. "Still, sir, I'm going on a date." She moved closer to Satter.

The man's mouth settled into a straight line. "Don't be following in your papa's footsteps, Rose." His eyes glimmered, as he turned to the boy. "You mind your manners, young man. You hear?"

Satter pulled at his collar. "Wouldn't think of doing anything else, sir," he croaked.

As soon as they were out of Mr. Alonzi's eyesight, Rose felt Satter relax, and she slipped her arm through his. Laying her head on his shoulder, she let out a long sigh.

Satter patted her hand. "I get a kick out of you, Rose."

"I bet you tell that to all the girls," she said.

She hugged his arm closer, and Satter began to whistle. When they emerged onto Main Street, the young man steered Rose through the doorway of the Hotel D'Hamburger.

Olive Blackburn greeted them in her enthusiastic way, blowing out a "howdy" and directing them to, "sit your hind ends anywhere." They slid into the only empty booth, near the kitchen door. Through the little square window, Rose could see Johnny's head, flanked by his remarkable ears, bobbing over a tall stack of plates.

Rose pulled a nickel out of her pocket and dropped it into the music box. "What should we play?"

Satter reached past her and pushed a button. "How 'bout *Satan Takes A Holiday*?"

They bounced their heads to the rhythm of Tommy Dorsey's energetic tune.

"Now don't start singing again, Olive!" Rose exclaimed, when she saw the waitress approach.

The woman, who had stopped in front of them with an open order book, looked crestfallen.

"You sure know how to spoil a mood." She cocked her head, licked the end of her pencil, and looked from face to face. "Whatcha want, kids?"

Satter ordered sliced meatloaf, whipped Idaho spuds and green beans, while Rose had fried fish and chips, since it was Friday. For dessert, they shared a scoop of chocolate ice cream from Jones-Enstrom Ice Cream Company.

It was said Chet Enstrom was thinking of opening a confectionary in addition to his ice cream company. Rose knew Mr. Enstrom experimented on confections in his basement. Frequently, when she walked by his house, a delicious aroma followed her down the street. Once, he'd popped out his front door and offered her a sample of his newest concoction. Something he called almond toffee. Like his ice cream, it was lip-smacking good.

As Satter noisily scraped the last of the cream out of the bowl, Rose dabbed at her mouth with a napkin.

"So, what are we doing tonight?"

"Care to dance?" Satter let the spoon clatter in the bowl. He stood up and pulled a coin purse out of his back pocket.

Rose glanced around the busy room. "Not in front of everybody!"

Satter laughed, carefully counting out change for the bill. "Not here, silly. At the Copeco."

"But, we have no way of getting there." Before they exited out the door, Rose waved at Olive. "Besides, I've never been to a dance before. I don't know how." She covered her ears when Satter whistled for a taxicab.

"Tonight, you're gonna learn, dear Rose."

The cab ride, which Rose enjoyed immensely, finally ended when it pulled onto a dirt lot in front of a big brick building.

Cars were parked hodgepodge everywhere, as if some giant toddler had tossed them in the air and left them where they'd landed. People streamed in and out of the lighted entrance like schools of fish.

Rose could see small groups of young men around some of the vehicles. They sat on running boards or leaned against long fenders, laughing and jostling each other with their elbows. Most tipped bottles of Tivoli Beer to their lips.

Curious, Rose looked at Satter, who shrugged.

"Can't drink or eat inside. Come on."

Rose followed Satter from the relative quiet of the parking lot into the dimly lit uproar of band music, dancing feet and a hundred shouting voices.

The wooden dance floor covered most of the room. A long continuous bench, crammed with cheering onlookers, encircled it. It seemed to Rose that there were as many people dancing as sitting.

The musicians played on a raised stage opposite the entrance. Over their heads, a banner draped across the wall introduced the Armand de Beque Band. Each band member looked sharp in a tuxedo and bowtie, shined shoes and neat haircut. The dapper bandleader, Armand de Beque, tapped the air with his baton in time to the music. Every once in a while he would turn and smile into the sea of moving bodies.

"They're good!" Rose shouted into Satter's ear.

He nodded enthusiastically. Before she knew it, she'd been dragged to the edge of the dance floor. Satter began flapping his arms and shaking his bottom, beckoning her to join him. She took his hand and was drawn into the swirling mass.

Rose watched the movements around her, smiling when a boy threw a girl over his shoulder. The girl landed neatly on her feet. It seemed like everyone was flipping or sliding or twirling. She looked helplessly at Satter. He shrugged as if to say, "Go with it!"

When the song ended, the bandleader made an announcement. "Okay, guys and dolls, it is time for the Big Apple!"

Rowdy cheers went up around Rose, and she clapped along, though she had no clue what the "Big Apple" was.

"You know what to do, so let's get this show on the road."

"Wait 'til you see this!" Satter pulled Rose behind him until they hooked up to a nearby circle of sweating boys and saddle-shoed girls.

Armand de Beque led everyone through a series of dance steps, whose names were foreign to Rose: Lindy Hop, Black Bottom, Shag, Suzi-Q, Charleston and a spraddle-legged move-ment called Posin'. She was familiar with Truckin', which she'd frequently seen done in the halls of Grand Junction High in between classes. On occasion she'd even joined the trendy queue.

"Praise Allah, Wiggle, wiggle, wiggle; Praise Allah, Wiggle and dance; do that stomp with lots of pomp and sweet romance!"

Rose leaned back and raised her hands heavenward, mimick-ing those around her.

"Truck to the right . . . and back again . . . stomp that left foot . . . swing it."

"Crazy!" Satter wheezed into Rose's ear, as the dance finally finished. "Uh, oh."

The tone in his voice caused Rose to follow his stare to a cou-ple, sitting on the bench. Rose recognized her friend, Mari, at once. She seemed to be arguing with a man sitting next to her.

"What is she doing here?" Satter took Rose's arm. "I better put a stop to this."

"Do you know Mari?"

"That's my sister. And it looks like stormy weather is about to erupt!"

"Will Mari be all right?"

"It ain't her I'm worried about!"

Just as they arrived, Mari shoved the man's shoulder and pulled back a fist. Satter grabbed it before it hit its target.

"Let go of me, you mealy-mouthed — "

"Tsk, Marietta, that ain't no way to talk to your kin." Satter grinned at her, and her face smoothed out.

"Course, I don't take kindly to sops being rude to my sister, either. What's the problem here?"

"I can take care of myself, thank you very much." Mari glared at the slight man, whose slicked back hair glistened under the dim lights. A nest of sweat beads had appeared above his thin lips when he'd seen Satter.

Mari had her fist in Cecil's face, again. "Get outta here, Cecil. You're disgusting!"

The man stood up and leaned close to Mari's face. "Yew'll be sorry ya said that! I'm th' best fella yew'll ever meet. One day it'll be plain as th' nose on yer face." Cecil's voice quivered, and Rose saw tears in his eyes. He turned and scowled at Satter. "She will, I tell ya."

"Go on now, and don't let me see you hasslin' my sister, again."

Rose felt sorry for the young man, as he wangled his way through the crowd. She could tell he had strong feelings for her friend.

"What happened?" Rose sat next to Mari on the bench.

"Wimpy made a pass at me." Mari snorted. "Like I'd fall for someone like him. Besides, he's hitched already!"

Mari looked from Rose to Satter. "You two know each other?"

"Satter's my date!"

"Sis, why aren't you taking care of Teddy? He was pretty sick."

Mari flicked her hand, dismissively. "Oh, he's fine now. I took him to Pa's."

Rose noticed Satter's doubtful face.

Apparently, so did Mari. "Say, wanna get outta here?"

Satter looked with longing at the dance floor, but gave in when Mari promised he could drive her car.

The three of them danced through the parking lot to the waning notes of *Sing, Sing, Sing*. The darkness furnished both pockets of giddy hilarity and hollow silence. Rose heard someone retching in the weeds, and a car accelerated out onto the road. She thought of Cecil.

The Packard's grill glowed under the bright half moon. Satter hopped into the driver's seat and cracked his knuckles before gripping the steering wheel.

"What a beaut she is, Sis! I'm gonna have one just like it after I've saved enough. Owning a car is living in a big way." He waggled his fingers for the key.

The engine came alive after he turned the key and pushed the starter button. Satter peered over his shoulder at Rose, eyebrows asking if he wasn't the cat's meow.

"Let's head to the cemetery," Mari suggested.

Rose hated cemeteries. "I know — let's not, and say we did!" she pleaded.

"Scaredy cat." Mari's teeth gleamed, as she smiled over the seat at Rose, then she punched Satter's shoulder. "Come on, boy, let's get some fun outta life!"

Satter put the car in reverse, the gears grinding until they finally dropped into place. After hitting the open road, the car glided over the pavement like it was riding on silk. The breeze blew through the open windows, and Rose felt like she was flying. She joined brother and sister as they sang.

"I'll take you home, Kathleen; across the ocean wild and wide; to where your heart has ever been; since first you were my bonny bride . . ."

Satter sang charmingly off key, but Rose thought it blended nicely with Mari's throaty alto and her soprano.

Five songs later, the Packard sailed over the bridge that spanned the Colorado River. A mile further, they drove past the Catholic section into the oldest part of the cemetery. Stones popped under the car's tires as they slowly traveled the dirt road. Satter slid to a stop and pulled the brake. The sudden silence was disconcerting to Rose.

They piled out of the car. Mari pointed to a brick mausoleum at the top of the hill in front of them.

"That's the final resting place of Junction's founder, George Crawford," she said in hushed tones. Rose stifled a giggle when Mari added, "Great place to eat watermelon and sneak a kiss on a date. Least, that's what I've been told."

Mari winked at the couple.

Rose hoped her own embarrassment wasn't noticeable, because even in the moonlight, Satter's ears were beet red.

"Shush, we don't want to wake the dead."

"Aw, kid, they're way beyond caring. Hey, I got an idea — Rose, scoot behind the wheel, and I'll give you your first driving lesson."

Rose was terrified at the idea, but Mari refused to be dissuaded. "You can't pull the wool over my eyes; you want to drive this baby as much as Li'l Brother."

The woman held the driver side door open and beckoned Rose to climb in. Rose gave her a long look, took a deep breath and scooted behind the steering wheel. Mari showed her how to start the car by turning the key, then pushing the starter button until the engine caught. Rose was feeling mighty proud of herself by then, and after grinding the gears into first, the car lurched forward.

"Hey, wait for me," Satter hollered. He hopped on the running board, hanging on while he pulled the door open. Mari squeezed close to Rose to make room for him.

"If Mr. Crawford had peeked out the door of his crypt that night, he would have thought the Keystone Kops had invaded his neighborhood. Mari let me drive all around the cemetery, and I did pretty well for my first time. I enjoyed it so much that I even forgot there were dead people everywhere. It was great fun.

"Of course, poor Otis Wagner probably didn't think it as funny as we did, when I nicked his headstone with the front bumper."

Rose's chuckle turned into a bout of coughing. Nick watched attentively until she finally caught her breath. She pulled a tissue out of her sleeve, and wiped her mouth.

"What an exhilarating time we had, and I'm grateful for Mari's insistence. She didn't know it, but that night she unleashed a spirit of adventure that's taken me all over the world."

"Nonna, how can one person, whom you knew for only a few weeks over sixty years ago, have such an impact on your life?" Nick dragged the heavy, wrapped bundle over to the broken ground and pulled at the rope's knot.

"Even in small ways, we touch one another's lives, Nicky. Haven't you ever caught a stranger's smile in the grocery store, and it suddenly turned a miserable day into one with great possibility?" Rose sighed. "Mari may have been unrefined and unwise at times, but she changed my life for the better."

After apologizing profusely to Otis Wagner, the trio stumbled up the hill toward George Crawford's tomb. They giggled and made so much noise, Rose thought his ghost would poke his head out and scare them away. This possibility sent a delicious shiver up her spine.

Scrambling onto a nearby boulder, they dangled their feet over the chasm that fell to the ground far below. The silver ribbon of the Colorado River severed them from the sparse city lights. From their high perch, Rose felt giddy.

"When you see the world from up here, it don't seem so bewildering," mused Mari.

"I'm surprised you're bewildered about anything, Sis. You seem to have the answer for every problem."

Mari ruffled her brother's hair. "Now, that ain't *entirely* true," she said, modestly.

"Sure it is. You've always come out on top, even with Pa." Satter turned to Rose. "No matter what mess she was in, she'd have Pa eating outta her hand in no time. Ain't that right, Sis?" He elbowed Mari, almost causing her to lose her seat on the rock.

"Don't be reckless, boy!" Mari readjusted her position and tucked her skirt under her legs again.

Satter didn't seem to notice her irritation. "Hey, Sis, tell Rose how you broke in Pa's mule. See, Pa had just purchased this gray-haired — "

"You gonna let *me* tell it?"

Satter grinned, sheepishly.

Mari focused her eyes on the distant past. "I'd just turned fourteen, and Pa had gone to town that morning. He was mad at me 'cause I'd been out the night before with a boy he didn't like. Course, Pa didn't like any boy that looked at me twice, which is probably why I married the first fella that asked for my hand. By then, I was more than ready for a life of my own. And — "

"Uh, Sis, the mule?"

Mari scowled at her brother. "I'm about to tell you, smarty. As I was saying, Pa had gone to town early, and I was still stinging from Pa's tongue lashing. As I ate my eggs and grits, I heard the mule kicking around in the corral. Pa had tried the past two mornings to harness the beast, but wasn't having any luck. That's when I got the idea I'd kill me two birds with one stone.

"I figured I'd knock that biggety mule down to size and restore Pa's faith in me again. So, I put on my biballs and boots and headed outside with a bridle swinging from my fingers.

"That mule and me sashayed around for nearly an hour, before I got fed up with his wahoo attitude."

A breeze swept up the side of the hill and cooled the night air. Rose moved closer to Satter, who placed his arm around her shoulder.

"Pa was due back," Mari continued, "and the situation didn't look like it was gonna change any time soon. I needed to think of something fast. Then a plan come to me.

"With his beady eyes watching my every move," Mari made sure she had her audience's attention before continuing, "I slowly laid the bridle on the ground. With my softest voice I began to sweet-talk him. Inch by inch, I stepped towards him, one hand out, the other behind my back. He must've suspected something because he got a bit skittery, but I just kept talking sweet. Soon I was close enough to smell his foul breath.

"Still cooin' like he was a baby, I bunched up my fist behind my back, and faster than you can say 'Bob's your uncle', I let him have it in the kisser!"

Satter convulsed with laughter. He rocked back and forth so hard, Rose was afraid he'd fall off the boulder and take her with him.

Satter wiped tears from his eyes. "Her hand hurt like the dickens for two weeks after, but when Pa came home, that derned mule had a bridle on him, even if he was out cold."

"Still got a scar." Mari held out her hand, and Rose saw a crescent-shaped scar on her knuckle. She also noticed a fresh cut on Mari's thumb and asked about it.

"One of my many 'admirers' cut me with his knife when I tried to take away his bottle of beer. He was hoary-eyed drunk, and I reckoned he'd had enough." She examined the wound, frowning. "He reckoned different."

"Sis, you need to find a higher class of fellas."

She stared balefully down at the city lights. "If I could find one in this crummy town I would, boy. It'd be right nice to settle down with a good fella."

Mari pulled a cigarette from a case and put it between her lips. After lighting it, she blew smoke circles into the air. It's acrid smell reached Rose's nose, and she sneezed.

"He better be rolling in the dough, too. I'd want me a Victorian house, with lots of bedrooms full of fancy furniture from Bannister's. Course, Teddy would get his own bedroom." Mari flicked an inch-long ash into the dark abyss. "There'd be a huge dining room, and the parlor would have a card table and a new Philco radio."

Rose sighed. "It sounds swell, Mari! What about you, Satter? Do you have a dream?"

Satter's face became serious, as a train whistle sounded across the river. Its mournful cry floated toward them on the breeze.

"Hear that train? Someday, I'm gonna climb on one of them new-fangled streamliners and ride it until I find my pot of gold. After I make my million, I'm gonna buy me a Rolls Royce and drive it past Pa's sorry door. Then he'll see Satter Simpson is a *somebody*."

"You're a *somebody* already, Satter. Just 'cause Pa don't acknowledge it, don't make it so," Mari said. She leaned forward. "Hey, kid, what's your wish?"

Rose thought for a moment. "Family is very important to Italians. A man is expected to work hard, own some property, tend a big vegetable garden. And if he grows roses, well, everyone knows he really loves his family." She sighed. "I wish Papa had grown roses."

"Why, he grew the swellest rose of all — you!" Satter drew the girl's hand to his chest.

Rose felt warm all over. "Why, thank you, Satter."

"What's the matter with him, anyway?" Mari asked.

"It's because of Mama. She died giving me birth, and he blames me."

"It wasn't your fault that happened!" Satter said.

Rose reluctantly withdrew her hand and stood up. "I know that, but it doesn't help to know it." She brushed the soil from her skirt and continued, "I've tried everything to make up for it, but I can't bring Mama back from the dead. And I can't make Papa love me!"

"Then you gotta move on. Some mules can't be broken." Mari crushed her cigarette into the dirt and tossed it over the edge. She stood up. "Not enough hours in the day to waste on a lost cause."

"I expect that's good advice for some folks, maybe even for me. But something keeps me from giving up." Rose stomped her foot. "Oh, why can't life be fair?"

Mari shrugged. "Who said it was supposed to be?"

No one could find an argument for that comment, so they began their descent to the car. The hill was so steep, the three had to slide on their backsides all the way down to the road. As they dusted off their clothes, a cloud closed over the moon, darkening the night.

"Any idea what time it is?" Mari yawned, as she patted her hair to see if her barrette was straight.

Satter pulled out a pocket watch and popped open the face. "Going on three o'clock in the morning. Oh, Rose, I shoulda gotten you home long before this. Will you get into trouble?"

"Don't worry about me," Rose said. She looked at her friends. "I had the time of my life tonight and, no matter what kind of trouble I get in, it was worth it!"

Mari waited in the Packard, as Satter walked Rose to her door. He kissed her on the cheek and whispered, "You're swell." Before getting in the car, he saluted Rose.

Life was grand.

Chapter Six

Rose threw back her covers, and put on her Sunday dress for Mass. After washing her face and braiding her hair, she warmed some water and brought Papa his coffee. His snores seemed extra loud, so she hoped he heard her wake up call.

Stepping onto the front porch, the memory of Satter's kiss came rushing back, and Rose's stomach lurched. She touched her cheek and it felt warm, as if the heat of his lips still lingered there, full of promise.

All the way to church, Rose had to keep steering her thoughts toward higher ground.

When Mass was over, everyone poured out the doors and milled around in front of the stairs. Mrs. Baldino stopped Rose in the foyer, inviting her to join the family for a picnic that afternoon on the Grand Mesa. She regretfully declined; she still had chores to do before Papa got home from the roundhouse. Mrs. Baldino muttered something under her breath about resting on the Lord's Day.

She said, louder, "I'll look in on you later, little one."

In the sunshine, Rose caught snatches of conversation: Mrs. Marasco praising the past week's Altar Guild luncheon, Mrs. Noonan introducing her cousin, Ida, who was visiting from California, and Mr. Mendicelli inviting Father Nick to supper on Wednesday.

The priest had a long line waiting to shake his hand, so Rose passed through the crowd and headed home. Crossing White Avenue, she waved to the McCabes, who came to church every Sunday in their horse and buggy.

The old couple didn't seem bothered by the stares their mode of transportation often elicited. No streamlined deluxe vehicles

for them, they'd declare, when questioned. About the only con-
cession to modern times they welcomed was displayed below the
carriage, where automobile tires had replaced the rough buggy
wheels.

As their horse clopped down the street, husband and wife sat
on the bench, dignified and serene. Mr. McCabe's arm cradled
his frail wife's shoulders, while she seemed to only have eyes for
his wrinkled, weathered face.

Rose watched them turn the corner, hoping she'd have such an
enduring love with her future husband. The subject of love
brought Satter to mind, and she happily allowed her thoughts to
dwell on him all the way home.

There was something different about the house when she
entered, but Rose couldn't quite put her finger on it. She changed
into her everyday dress, sliced tomatoes and cheese for lunch, and
had cleaned up before it dawned on her.

Papa's coffee cup.

Every morning, before Papa went to work, he placed his cup
on the table to be washed. Today, it was nowhere to be seen.

Thinking her father had forgotten the cup in his bedroom, she
opened his door. When she saw him still in bed, she rushed to his
side. His grizzled face was flushed and his breathing shallow.

"Papa!" Rose shook her father, but his eyes remained closed.
She'd once seen Rollie, Mrs. Baldino's youngest, look like this,
and knew her father was very sick. She didn't know what to do.
Dr. Munro made house calls, but they didn't even have a chicken
to trade for his services.

Pumping cold water over a cloth, Rose dabbed Papa's forehead with it. His groans alarmed her, and she felt she must do
something quick, or he would die. Mrs. Baldino was picnicking
on the Mesa, so Rose knew there was no help nearby. Mari
came to mind.

"Papa, I'll be back soon."

Rose ran all the way to her friend's bungalow. She pounded on
the screen door, but no one answered.

"Oh!" Rose kicked the doorjamb, and then covered her mouth to muffle her frustration.

"What's up, kid? You're gonna wake all these fine, hard-working ladies with your commotion."

Rose whirled around and saw Mari standing in the doorway of a house across the alley, wearing a dust cap and flowered apron over her street clothes. Rose ran to her friend.

"Papa's sick. Please, Mari, could you come?"

"Well, let me see if Her Majesty can spare me, okay?"

Rose paced the alley, stirring up the dirt. Finally Mari came out and slammed the screen door shut. Rose froze when she heard Emma Splott's curses from inside the house. They splintered the sleepy afternoon air.

"Don't mind her," Mari snorted. "She's been in a nasty mood for sixty-some years."

"I'm truly sorry to take you away from your chores, but I think Papa needs to go to the hospital. He's hardly breathing and he's very hot."

"Better take the car."

Moments later, they pulled up in front of the house.

At Papa's bedside, Mari tsked. "Looks bad, kid."

With a grunt, she hoisted the man over her shoulder like he was a sack of potatoes. Spittle dribbled from his slack mouth, as she trudged to the car and settled him in the front seat. Rose climbed into the back and dabbed her father's face with a damp cloth.

"His breath smells like he ate supper with the scavengers," Mari said, rolling down her window.

"Mari!"

"Now, don't get your nose outta joint. Don't mean nothing by it." Mari started the car. "Say, kid? Just where *is* the hospital?"

St. Mary's Hospital, run by the Sisters of Charity of Leavenworth, spanned the southeast corner of Eleventh and Colorado. Its latest wing had been completed in 1924, but the hospital was still described as "innovative" by small town standards. Mrs. Baldino, who sometimes volunteered at the hospital, told Rose that it housed the first elevator in the area, though the new-fangled convenience seemed to have a mind of its own. It often would stop between floors and, once, had plummeted into the basement when it slipped a cog. No one had been seriously hurt but, anymore, the sisters crossed themselves and looked heavenward before stepping foot in it.

The one and only time Rose had been to the hospital was on Tonsil Day. She remembered waiting in a long line, when she was seven, to have her tonsils taken out. After that excruciating experience, she had fervently hoped never to darken its doorways again.

Mari screeched to a halt in front of the entrance, and threw her door open. Rose scrambled out of the vehicle and rushed to her father's side. She tried to extract him, but Mari shouldered her out of the way.

"I'll carry him," she said. "You'll hurt yourself."

Rose opened her mouth to protest, but Mari gave her a forbidding look. Resigned, Rose stood back.

At that moment, a hearse pulled in front of the Packard, and numerous nuns dressed in black habits piled out of the long interior.

Rose smiled at Mari's raised eyebrows, and explained. "Mr. Callahan, the undertaker, drives the sisters to and from the church. He's Catholic."

"Hmm." With effort, Mari readjusted Rose's father on her shoulder and turned toward the hospital's entrance.

Two men, carrying a stretcher, came out to meet them, and Mari seemed relieved to turn her burden over to them. One of the nuns who had gotten out of the hearse held the door open. Rose often saw her at church services and knew her name was Sister Mary Perpetua Quigley, the Mother Superior and administrator of St. Mary's. She thanked the nun as she hurried after the stretcher.

Soon, Papa was ushered into a small, sparsely furnished room. Rose held her father's hot hand, while Mari sunk down on the only chair. The Mother Superior went to summon Dr. Munro, who was making his Sunday rounds. She returned with the doctor and then waited in the doorway in case she was needed.

"Hello, Rose." Dr. Munro touched the girl's shoulder before glancing curiously at Mari.

"Howdy, Doc."

"Afternoon, Marietta. How is that youngster of yours?" Dr. Munro clicked open his black bag and pulled out a stethoscope. He unbuttoned his patient's shirt.

"He's a blue-eyed wonder, Doc. Can't keep that kid down for long."

"Good, good." The doctor's voice became distant as he listened to his patient's heartbeat. He performed several other mysterious procedures before finally snapping his bag shut. He indicated that everyone should join him in the hallway.

"Rose, we better quarantine Sante, just to be sure. It looks like pneumonia, so we need to take care." His pale eyes peered kindly at her through wire rim glasses. "Will you be all right alone?"

Dr. Edward Ernest Hale Munro reminded Rose of Daddy Warbucks, with his cherubic face, smooth baldhead, and ready smile. He had delivered Rose and, according to Mrs. Baldino, had valiantly tried to save her mother's life. Mrs. Baldino said he'd cried as he'd placed the sheet over her face. Whenever Rose met the doctor on the street, his features fell into lines of compassion, as if that memory was still just below the surface.

"I'll be fine on my own, Doctor."

Mari leaned close to Rose. "And I'll keep an eye on her, too."

Sister Mary Perpetua said, "He might be here for a while, child."

"Can I visit him?"

"Why don't we see how he progresses?"

The doctor's news frightened me, Nicky. In those days there were no antibiotics or fancy medicines. The chances of anyone surviving pneumonia were small. The illness was called the "old man's best friend" because it was a mild way to die — you just simply ran out of breath. But, since Papa was young, my hope for his getting better was strong.

Rose spent the rest of the afternoon at home. Mari dropped her off, saying she had to get back to "cleaning the castle."

Rose immediately put a large kettle of water on the stove. After it came to a boil, she added lye soap and steeped Papa's bedding in it. Then she scoured every surface and crevice in each room, until her hands were red and raw.

Mrs. Baldino stopped by early evening. She'd already heard about Papa, as news spread quickly through Little Italy. She handed Rose a basket with still-bubbling lasagna and crusty rolls nestled in the folds of cloth. Kissing Rose's forehead, she promised to look in on her the next day. Rose gave the woman a wan smile, then closed the door. Leaning her back against it, she let her shoulders slump.

Everything seemed out of kilter. Neither Mrs. Baldino's concern, nor the delicious aroma of tomato, spices, and melted cheese coming from the basket helped soothe the strange ache in Rose's belly. She felt no inclination to eat, but sat down and made herself pick up a fork. Papa's empty chair stared at her, as she poked her food.

After she washed up, Rose wandered into Papa's room. The window was open, and fresh bedding scented the dusky evening air.

On his starched pillowcase lay the small leather-bound book Rose had found when she'd flipped over his heavy down mattress that afternoon. The book had flown across the room landing with its dark covers splayed on the floor.

Curious, she had picked it up, and was startled to see her mother's name, *Maria Rosa,* on the cover. She'd run her fingers lightly over the worn gold-stenciled letters and realized this was her mother's journal. *Why has Papa never shown me this?*

Rose hadn't known what to do. Perhaps, in her hands were answers to many questions, but if Papa knew she had found it — he had hidden it, after all — he'd be very upset. The thought of Papa's anger had caused her to drop the book on his nightstand and leave the room. All afternoon as she washed and pressed his sheets, the book called to her. She had wrestled with the temptation to look at it while she made his bed, but after the bed was made, she'd carefully placed it on his pillow, unopened.

Now, as the sun descended in the sky, Rose stood in her father's doorway. She was drawn to the book like a moth to a flame. Sitting on the edge of his bed, she picked it up. Brilliant corals and pinks splashed against the jagged profile of the nearby cliffs, reflecting off the wall behind Rose. The girl basked in the sunset's warmth momentarily, and then made a decision.

As Papa's room darkened, she took the book and carried it to the kitchen table. She sat down and stared at it. She lit the lamp. She tapped her fingers. She glanced at Papa's doorway. Slowly, she slid her hand toward the front cover.

Rose smoothed the crisp pages, lifting them to her nose. A musty, earthy smell wafted up, and she breathed deeply as if breathing in the very soul of her mother. Something dropped into her lap. A dried rose. Scooping it onto her palm, she caught its faraway fragrance.

Why had Mama saved it? Had Papa given it to her?

Finding the first entry, Rose saw the date was four months after her mother's marriage to Papa.

In Italian it began, *"My beloved Sante . . ."*

For several pages, her mother declared her love for Papa, and Rose blushed at the details and strength of her sentiments. Still, she couldn't put the journal down.

One passage caught her by surprise.

"I miss your beautiful voice," her mother wrote.

She didn't know Papa could sing. It was apparent there was more to her father than Rose supposed. It became apparent, too, that her mother's family had been wealthy in the Old Country. She spoke of land and vineyards, of merchants and goods. Rose looked around their stark house and wondered where all her mother's wealth went. Her question was answered a page later when the dreaded Black Hand was mentioned. *Poor Mama.*

More than anything, Maria Rosa wrote of joining her new husband in America. *"In the land of opportunity, our little family will be safe and hopeful."*

Little family? Rose realized her mother must have been with child when she wrote this.

"Mama's words were like mother's milk to me. You see, Nicky, there had never been a natural weaning between us. A part of me had

remained a babe longing for her mama's breast. Such emptiness I felt without her."

Nick threw his shovel on the ground and peeled off his gloves. Kneeling in front of his grandmother, he cried, "How could you live without her, Nonna?"

"As with the death of any loved one, Nicky, what choice do we have but to live without them? The real question is how will we handle the loss? Will we bury our pain in drink or hate or blame, surely ruining our lives and the lives of others? Or will we embrace death's sword so it can lance our wounds? Only one choice leads to healing and wholeness."

"But — "

Rose held up a hand. "I know it takes a great deal of courage and wisdom to embrace the sword, Nicky. Papa drank his life away, and I spent my childhood trying to prove I was worthy of his love. I was so confused. I felt both of my parents had deserted me. But, God had not. He let me find my mother's journal just when I needed it the most."

"I'm glad God came to your rescue, Nonna." Nicky laid his head on his grandmother's lap. He felt so tired. "But I don't think He can help me."

With a gentle finger, Rose brushed a lock of her grandson's hair back in place. "You will survive this, Nicky. Katharine's death will change you, but you must trust God. One day you will have peace."

"I'd rather have Katharine!"

"Papa felt that way, too." Rose's voice became tender. "You don't want to follow in his footsteps, do you?"

Nick reached into his pocket and felt the vial of pills. *No, there's another way,* he thought.

Rose's eyelids had grown heavy. She laid her head on the table, her cheek resting against the pages of her mother's journal.

When she awoke, sunlight filled the room. Papa! All of the antipathy she'd felt for her father over the last few weeks disappeared in one thought. *Mama hadn't loved a monster; she'd loved a man.* Yes, he was pathetic and he was sick, but he deserved to be loved, even now. If Mama were here, she'd make sure he got well. Rose felt her mother's spirit close, and it energized her.

"Father Nick!" Rose caught the priest just as he was leaving the sanctuary after early Mass. She'd run all the way to the church, and had to catch her breath before she could speak again.

"Running a little late for work, my girl? Here, sit down and collect yourself." Father Nick sat on the steps and motioned for Rose to sit next to him.

"Papa fell ill yesterday," Rose said between gasps, "and he's at the hospital." She told him what happened after she got home from Mass. "They won't let me see him yet, so could you go for me, Father? Could you tell him that I love him?" Rose gripped the priest's sleeve. "I'm afraid he's going to die."

"Of course I'll visit Sante." The priest stood up. "Now, don't worry. He's in good hands with the capable sisters, and God is watching over him, too."

"Today, Father? Can you visit him right now?" She held her breath, waiting for his answer.

The priest rubbed his chin and looked thoughtfully at the girl. "No time like the present, I always say."

"Then, may I *please* go with you? I'll stay out of the way. I promise."

"Hmm." He clasped his hands behind him and rocked back and forth, pretending to mull the question over. Amusement sparkled in his eyes. "Let me inform Sister Mary Bernadine I'll be borrowing you for a while, and then we'll take a taxi."

Rose watched Father Nick disappear through the office door. Moments later, he returned carrying a prayer book. They waited quietly together, until the taxi pulled up in front of them.

When they arrived, Sister Juletta, a large, red-faced Irish woman, followed them up the stairs. She carried a potted arrangement of blood-red chrysanthemums. Directing Rose to wait in the hallway by the stairwell, she bustled after Father Nick into Papa's room. Rose saw the nun place the flowers on a table near his bed.

From her chair, Rose could see a slice of sunshine angle from the window and touch her father's face. It looked gray and lifeless. For a moment, she had an unsettling vision of her father in a coffin.

She watched, as Father Nick draped a purple stole around his neck and opened his prayer book. After anointing her father's forehead with oil, the priest began his prayer. "Through this holy anointing, may the Lord, in His love and mercy, help . . ."

Though the words were in Latin, Rose was comforted. She squeezed her eyes shut and added her own prayers.

Suddenly, beautiful singing filled the hallway.

Rose blinked open her eyes. Had God sent angels in Papa's time of need? The ethereal sound drifted around her, and she jumped up, plastering her back against the wall. Wildly, she looked up and down the hall but saw no luminous glow, no flashing of iridescent wings. Yet, the song grew stronger.

Goodness, she wondered, *what does one do when meeting angels?* She took several deep breaths for she was feeling a bit light-headed by now.

Just as she thought she was going to burst with anticipation, or worse yet, faint and miss the whole experience, Sister Mary Perpetua Quiqley turned the corner. She was humming the same song as the angels.

The nun stopped when she saw Rose. "Have you just seen a ghost, child? Goodness, your eyes are as round as dinner plates!"

"I, I – " Rose gulped. Though the nun had quit humming, she could still hear the singing. "Do you hear them, Sister?"

Sister Mary Perpetua tilted her head and listened. "The dear sisters' voices are lovely, aren't they? They do carry up the stairwell from the chapel."

Rose snapped her mouth shut, sinking down in her chair. The nun beamed at the girl before swishing into Papa's room.

Father Nick came out, and mistook Rose's dazed look for concern. "He's a little better today, child. The Mother Superior assures me your father's on the mend."

Sister Juletta, following close behind the Mother Superior, trilled, "Sure, and I hope me mums will warm the dear man's heart when he wakens." Both nuns inclined their heads and glided away.

Rose burst into tears.

"My dear girl, what's wrong?"

Frankly, Rose didn't know why she was weeping. She couldn't help herself. She just felt overwhelmed. Maybe it was the exquisitely painful feelings she had for Satter, or discovering Mama's journal, or that there were no angels.

Maybe, it was Papa's close call with death. Why, if she hadn't looked in his bedroom, he might have died! Then, where would she be? Where would *he* be? She began to wail.

Rose took the handkerchief Father Nick held out to her and scrunched it fiercely to her eyes. Between sobs, she asked, "What if Papa had died, Father? Where would he have gone? He won't attend Mass, he doesn't pray to God, he *hates* me. He's hell-bound, for sure!"

"That's a reasonable fear, Rose, but only God can see the true state of Sante's heart." He placed his hands on Rose's shoulders and looked into her eyes. "Many people are praying for him. You must trust the Lord, who is faithful to keep your father safe during this dark time."

With her whole heart, Rose wanted to believe the priest. She sniffed. "Well, if you say so," she said.

"I do, indeed. Now, I believe we have a taxi waiting."

When Rose got home that afternoon, she was surprised to find Mari standing in the doorway. She was a sight. Every bit of the woman, from her dark curls to her white sneakers, was covered in a thick dusting of flour.

"That ol' busybody next door was gonna summon the cops, but I persuaded her to let me fix you supper." Mari jerked her head toward Mrs. Baldino's house. A white shower sprinkled onto the porch. "Made me feel about as welcome as a skunk at a tea party."

Mari left splashy white footsteps as she walked toward the kitchen. Flour flurried outward, as she turned and extended her hand with a flourish.

"Ta da!"

Rose's delight turned to dismay, as her eyes glided from the vase of pink roses that adorned the tabletop to the chaos behind it.

It looked like every pan in the house was piled in the sink. The large pot Rose had used to disinfect Papa's bedding was bubbling over on the stove. Vegetable peelings trailed along the side of the counter, and a sack of flour had exploded, explaining Mari's ghostly appearance.

Obviously pleased with her efforts, Mari beckoned for Rose to sit at the table. With a spoon, she dug into a pan on the counter and plopped a portion of its contents onto a plate. She placed it in front of the girl.

Rose forced her eyes downward and gulped.

"Why, this looks, um, real tasty." She couldn't quite make out what exactly *this* was, but gingerly stabbed at the gooey, greenish slab with her fork.

Mari hovered at her elbow with an air of expectancy.

"Mmm, what is this?"

"Do you like it?"

"Sure, Mari, but really, what is it?" Rose's mouth began to pucker and she blinked tears away.

"Family recipe. Zucchini and summer squash jambalaya. The grocer was out of summer squash, so I used lemons instead. Don't make too much difference, I suspect. They're both yella." Mari clapped her hand to her mouth. "I forgot the noodles! Homemade," she called over her shoulder, "just like you Eye-tal-ians do it."

From the pot on the stove, Mari swirled a glob of long white tendrils onto a serving fork.

She blew on the dripping mass as she carried it to the table. Just as it passed over Rose's lap, it slipped off. Rose scraped her chair back and quickly stood up, barely avoiding the mess, as it slumped to the floor.

"Oops, that ain't supposed to happen."

Rose couldn't help it. She started to laugh. "We *Eye*-talians prefer our pasta on our plates, thank you."

Rose reached down and pulled out a noodle. She blew on it before tossing it Mari's way. It stuck to the woman's nose for a second, and then dropped to the shelf of her bosom.

"I believe you was aiming for this!" A noodle landed in Rose's hair.

Squealing, the fight ensued. After a while, the two friends slid to the floor and leaned against the wall. Giggling, they surveyed the mayhem. Amazingly, the only thing left unscathed was the vase of pink roses.

"I'm glad Papa's not coming home soon, or Sheriff Lumley would have him behind bars for double murder," Rose said.

"We need a fire hose."

Rose raised one eyebrow.

"We could wash the walls down, lickety split."

Rose grinned. "You do have interesting ways of solving predicaments, Mari. I wish I could be as creative as you. But," she slapped her thighs, "you're right. We better clean up before this mess hardens, or Papa will have a fit."

Mari reached over and pulled a noodle off Rose's shoulder. "Why do you stay with the lugoon, kid?" She flung the noodle toward the kitchen. "I'm not trying to be a wisenheimer, but you got work, you're schooled and you're right pretty. Why, you could hitch up with dern near any fella you'd like and make a nice home for yourself. You should tell that no-good pa of yours to take a hike!"

Rose stirred uncomfortably. "That's not how things are done in Little Italy. Family always comes first. My community — and God — expects me to respect and love Papa, even if he's difficult."

Mari snorted. "Your pa don't deserve a daughter like you. It'd be a favor, mind you, if this 'God' you speak of went ahead and relieved you of that particular burden."

"Bite your tongue, Mari!" Rose shifted to face her friend. "Papa's not perfect, but nobody is. Not me, not you, not Papa."

"If you ask me, some people are more imperfect than others," Mari grumbled. "Your pa should be horsewhipped for what he does to you." She shook a fist at Papa's bedroom door.

Rose laughed. "Mari, it wouldn't surprise me if you had slugged the doctor that delivered you. It's just the way you are, and I think you're swell." She took Mari's fist and gently uncurled her fingers. "Some situations call for action, but there are times when you just need to sit tight and wait."

"What in blue blazes are you waiting for?"

"A miracle," Rose replied, simply.

"Hmm. I don't rightly believe in fairy tales."

"You mean you don't believe in God?" This had never occurred to Rose, and it disturbed her.

"I reckon there's gotta be someone in charge of this worthless world. Not too sure I'd take a liking to him, though. Seems to me, he'd have more say in the way things are run down here, don't you think?"

"Well, this isn't Heaven, Mari, and people don't always want to abide by the rules. The world's problems aren't God's fault. They are ours. I know God wishes better things for us — He loves us, after all. And, like Father Nick said during Sunday's sermon, God has ways of bringing good out of bad situations. That's why I believe in miracles."

"Mighty naive of you, kid." Mari stood and pulled Rose up. "So — you think I'm swell, huh?"

Rose gave her a quick hug. "More than you know. You're my best friend, Mari. Thank you for fixing me supper — it really cheered me up. Now," she looked around, "where did that dishrag go?"

"I know a fella that's a fireman . . . ."

Chapter Seven

*A*t first, Rose worried about her father all the time. Since she was not allowed to see Papa, she relied on Father Nick's reports of his progress. By week's end, he was doing much better, and Rose's concerns began to dwindle. Once, the priest offered to take the girl to the hospital, but she hastily put him off. Papa was in good hands, she told him, and the sisters didn't need her in the way.

The real reason she didn't want to see him was, since Papa had left, Rose was experiencing a freedom she'd never known before. She felt like a bird that had finally found its wings. Unfettered from her father's petrifying presence, she flew joyously and with delight. She was too enamored with her new independence to let a visit with Papa bring her crashing down to earth.

Over the following weeks, little-explored facets of her personality began to emerge, and she voiced long-oppressed opinions to anyone who would listen.

She liked the color purple, Shirley Temple, pie-eating contests (particularly peach), bingo and President Roosevelt. She disliked winter, Clark Gable (he looked too much like Papa), and the fact that boys could wear blue jeans and girls couldn't. She loved a good joke and despised eggplant.

These musings often had Mrs. Baldino pursing her lips in disapproval, but conversations with Mari and Satter produced rolling eyes and good-natured grins. Father Nick remained unruffled but amused, and even cheered the girl on.

Rose could hardly stand to be at home. It reminded her that Papa would soon return to clip her wings. At first, she ignored her daily chores. She thumbed her nose at her unmade bed and unwashed dishes as she bounced out the door in search of adventure. Old-fashioned Catholic guilt, and Mrs. Baldino's frequent admonitions finally convinced Rose to resume her home front duties. But, the wonderful world outside called to her, so even while her hands worked, her mind wandered.

Something Rose still enjoyed was cooking, although cooking for one was lonely. She thought of inviting Satter and Mari over, but felt sure Mrs. Baldino would chase Satter down the street with a rolling pin if he came near her unchaperoned. So Rose suggested the threesome have picnic suppers at the park.

After experiencing Mari's culinary talents, Rose offered to make the meals. Most times, they simply shared thick slices of Mrs. Strange's homemade bread with generous helpings of churned butter and apple jelly. Fresh, cold milk, drunk from mason jars, topped the meal off. The fare was humble, but the trio thought it most delicious.

The park offered the perfect backdrop as Rose, Satter and Mari's friendship grew. Sometimes, Johnny would join the trio. Around them, mothers visited while their children shouted to one another through "tom walkers" made from empty tomato cans, or played kick the can or hide-and-go-seek. Every once in a while, a homemade go-cart would zoom by, the driver's face alight with youthful joy.

Lying on a blanket under a canopy of leaves, the friends would discuss current events, such as the first ominous rustlings of war in Europe, the newest movie, or the town's sewer problems. They'd reminisce about the "good ol' days" or watch the flowing clouds and daydream about the future. When the setting sun stretched its golden orange fingers through the elm trees, Satter would roll up the blanket, and everyone headed homeward.

"Where have you been staying, lately?" Rose asked Satter, one evening. As they started walking, she hooked her arm through the young man's. Mari reapplied her lipstick before catching up to them.

"Most of the time, I bed down on my friend, Joe's, porch. Easier than walking five miles to Pa and Ma's. They have a fella staying with 'em right now, though I haven't seen hide nor hair of him — "

"That'd be Cecil." Mari snorted the name like a flea had suddenly got caught in her throat. "Pa gave him your bed 'cause he needs the moola." She rubbed two fingers together.

Rose tried to think why that name sounded familiar, and then remembered the slender fellow at the Copeco. The one who liked Mari.

"Well, if it wasn't him, it'd be someone else. I don't get it, Sis. Why didn't they just let me stay in Oklahoma with the Olsons? Mr. Olson made me feel like one of his own, and I liked the hardware store, especially the tractors." Satter did a fair rendition of a tractor engine running.

Mari rolled her eyes and grinned at Rose. "Well, I don't know why, boy, but I'm sure glad you came." She patted Rose's back. "And I'm sure this girl is happy, too."

Rose couldn't agree more.

The next Wednesday, Rose visited Papa. Father Nick had brought her, and he gently pushed her through the doorway before disappearing down the stairwell. Several pillows propped up her father's slumped form and his hands were slack across his stomach. She watched his slow breathing for a moment, gathering courage to approach his side.

At their little house in Little Italy, he'd been a bogeyman whose presence petrified her. In this benign setting, he didn't look at all fearsome. He seemed withered, like someone had ripped the stuffing out of him. Rose suddenly felt pity for her father. She tiptoed toward him.

"You just now coming to visit your papa on his sickbed?" Her father's dark eyes swiveled toward her.

Rose's step faltered. "I — I wanted to give you time to get better, Papa. The sisters said you needed your rest."

She leaned forward to kiss his brow, but he moved his head away. Rose felt a white-hot burst of anger and almost stormed out of the room, but Mama's love for him whispered softly in her ear. She felt her anger ebb. Pulling the nearby chair close to his side, she laid a hand on his arm.

"I've missed you Papa." Rose saw his jaw relax a little. "I cleaned the whole house, too, in-including your bedroom. When you come home, everything will be spic and span."

"Humph," was all he said.

The room became quiet. Rose noticed a new bouquet of flowers had been set on the table. A burst of orange zinnias this time. Rose reached out and touched a petal.

"Why didn't you tell me about Mama's journal, Papa?"

Her father's sigh was long and quavering. "My *bell'un*. Maria Rosa was twenty when she sailed to America. And six months with child."

"With *me*, Papa."

"I'd saved enough money to buy her a house, and when Maria Rosa arrived, it was the happiest day of my life!" Her father wiped away a tear with the palm of his hand.

"The trip was hard on her. Her family had suffered greatly before she'd left. The Black Hand had stolen all that they owned, and it broke her heart to leave her parents in poverty. When she arrived, by train, she was very ill. Dr. Munro put her in bed until her time. Only — " Papa's face crumpled.

"She died giving birth to me."

Her father looked out the window and nodded.

"I'm still here, Papa. Mama died, but you have me. Doesn't that matter?" Rose gripped her father's hand.

Tears flowed down her father's cheeks, unchecked. "She was all I ever wanted."

Rose sat back in astonishment.

"Papa, do you realize what you're saying? That I mean nothing to you!" Rose jumped up and stood at the foot of the bed.

"Look at you! Don't you think others have lost a loved one? Do *they* lie down and wait for death? Do *they* drink until they're stupid? Do *they* destroy whatever good thing God has given to comfort them in their grief?

"Look at me, Papa! I'm here. I've always been here, waiting for your love," she stumbled over her words, "waiting to give you love." Rose clasped her hands to her chest. "I still am."

The man turned his face to the wall.

As a child, Rose had often played in an empty field near her house. One day, while chasing a grasshopper, she'd suddenly been engulfed in a dust devil. One moment, the spring sky had been a cornflower blue, the next, an inky fury. The tornado of dust and debris had immobilized her with terror and when it had broken free, she'd run away from it.

As Rose stared at her father's stiff back, a similar fury engulfed her. This time, she embraced it.

"I want you to cut my hair." Rose held up her only pair of scissors, the ones she used to dismember roasting chickens.

"Whoa, kid, I ain't no good at that. Besides, why you wanna cut that gorgeous mane off?" Mari tugged on a lock of Rose's hair.

Rose pulled away, and said, "I just do, and if you won't cut it, I'll find someone else who will."

"I can see you're serious 'bout this. Tell you what, Her Majesty's all thumbs where her own mess is concerned, but I've seen her trim up her girls nifty. What say we go and ask her to help?"

Emma Splott's house, across the alley, was three times bigger than Mari's tiny cabin, with several rooms, including a kitchen. The flowered carpet nearly covered the whole floor, with runners that extended through two wide doorways. Rose could see a tall bedpost through one door and what looked like a water closet through the other. A peculiar odor permeated the air, and though Rose couldn't place the smell, she found it vaguely unpleasant.

Victorian furniture squatted heavily around the front room: a red velvet divan, an ornate dining table with two needlepoint chairs, a roll-top desk and a carved sideboard. Everything abutted the walls leaving a clear area for Emma's wheelchair, which sat like a throne between brocade-curtained windows. It seemed like every inch of wall space was crammed with framed pictures, stick-pinned postcards, and dark shelves of dusty knickknacks.

A hipbath sat in the corner nearest the kitchen, a radio console nearby. The volume was up, and Rose heard a male announcer report, "You're listening to KFXJ, your local radio station." Soothing music soon filled the room.

"Evening, Emma. You remember Rose, doncha?"

Rose nodded at the old woman, taking in the feathered boa that wrapped several times around her knotty neck. It was bright pink and matched the fire-breathing dragons on her black satin robe. She was leaning on a crutch and peering at Rose with intense interest.

"Sit down, sit down, dearie. Welcome to our humble," here she cackled with obvious pride, "home."

Like the first time she'd met the woman, her voice struck Rose as strange. It seemed a jumble of many inflections, and she could not quite figure out just where Emma hailed from.

She overheard the woman whisper to Mari, "Brought us a new prospect, eh?" The diamond-studded tooth flashed briefly in Rose's direction.

Rose looked at Mari to see if Emma was joking.

Her friend put a protective arm around Rose and said, "She ain't no prospect, Emma. She just wants you to cut her hair. Can you do it? I'll pay you." Mari held out a quarter, which the old woman grabbed. She reached inside her robe, and Rose was horrified to realize Emma had deposited the coin in her brassiere.

"Why, we'd be happy to oblige."

Emma hobbled over to the divan and, with some difficulty, settled down onto the deep-set cushion. She hitched up her robe, revealing her disfigured foot. Rose avoided looking at the foot by pretending interest in a framed picture on the wall above Emma's head.

"Mari, pull a chair around so our Rose can sit. And," she flung a finger toward a pile of newspapers haphazardly stacked beside the screen door, "lay some of those underneath."

Rose sat sideways, while the old woman raked her fingers through Rose's hair. It was then the girl realized where the peculiar smell that filled the house came from. It was Emma's breath.

"Who do you want to look like, dearie? Ginger Rogers, Claudette Colbert, maybe Jeanette McDonald? We can make you look like a star!"

"How 'bout Joan Crawford? Her dark features — "

"I want to look like Mari." Rose smiled at her friend's puzzled, but pleased, expression.

"Rather fond of our girl, eh?"

A wheezy, rumbling sound erupted from Emma when Rose presented her kitchen shears. It took a moment for the girl to realize the old woman was laughing.

"These will never do. Mari, fetch my — I mean, bring us our scissors." Emma fished around in the folds of her robe and pulled out a tiny key. "They're in the desk, and be quick about it."

Nonna shook her head. "That voluminous brassiere was like Mary Poppins' carpetbag. You never knew what she was going to pull out of it. I learned at the trial that, once, Shantytown had been raided by the police in an effort to clean up the area. Somehow Emma was missed in the roundup, but she wasn't about to sit around and let her girls "stew in a cell," as she put it.

"In the middle of the night, she made an unscheduled appearance at the jailhouse. The officer on duty that night said she'd hobbled up to his desk and pulled a six-shooter out of that brassiere, demanding her girls be released." Rose shook her head. "There's no denying that Emma Splott was one of a kind!"

While Mari looked for the scissors, Emma told Rose about a famous person she ("we") had met.

"So Mr. Crosby says to us — Mari, what's taking you so long? Well, it's about time."

When Mari handed the scissors to Emma, Rose noticed her mouth was pinched and her eyes disconcerted. She looked like she was going to say something, but then she didn't.

Emma held her palm up. "Ahem."

Mari hesitated, and then dropped the tiny key into it. In a wink, it disappeared into the hidden recesses of her robe.

"So, as we were saying, Mr. Crosby says to us . . ."

One incredible story became the springboard for another. She spoke with great gestures, carving the air with her red-tipped nails. Once, Rose dodged the points of the scissors, which threatened to nick her cheek. Rose doubted much of what Emma said was true, but she was entertaining. *A curious creature, indeed.*

Every few minutes, Rose would glance down at the floor, aghast at the accumulating mass of walnut brown hair. Sometime between snips, a hair iron had been heated, and when Emma was finished cutting, her short tresses were styled into waves. Mari used the barrette from her own hair to put the finishing touch on Rose's transformation.

"Are you ready, dearie?" Emma gave Rose a handheld mirror to see the final results.

The girl was speechless as she gazed at her reflection. Then she looked at Mari. "Do you think Satter will like it?"

"He'd be a moron, if he didn't," she exclaimed, gathering Rose in a hug. "You look beautiful, kid!"

The next day, Father Nick complimented Rose on her new hairdo, and even Sister Mary Bernadine stated how becoming she looked. When the church bells rang at noontime, Rose rushed to J.C. Penney's to meet Satter. She couldn't wait to see his reaction.

The thought occurred to her that he might not like the change. She suffered a slight dip in confidence at the thought, but shrugged her doubts away. There was nothing to be done, if he didn't. Besides, who wouldn't like it? Her father's face appeared, but she shooed the image away. *Who cares what he thinks? Certainly not me.*

Satter was still waiting on a customer when she arrived. She watched him while he worked with the matronly woman, his voice respectful and demeanor attentive. Rose felt her heart swell with adoration. What a good man!

When he handed the woman her package, Rose quietly came up behind him. "I'd like nineteen pairs of shoes, please." She tried to make her voice sound low and throaty, like Greta Garbo.

Satter turned around with surprise still forming on his mouth. When he saw Rose, his jaw dropped.

Rose giggled. "Cat got your tongue?"

Satter gulped, then put his hands on her shoulders. He turned her one way then the other, whistling long and low.

"Hello-o, gorgeous!"

"You like it?"

"Mmm-mmm."

Rose enjoyed the many sideways looks her companion gave her, as they walked to the park. It was like Satter was seeing her for the first time again, and she felt flattered. Even beautiful, like Mari had said.

Satter only had half an hour to eat, so when they'd finished, Rose walked with him back to the store. He seemed reluctant to let her leave, which pleased her. Lately, thoughts of a future together with the young man filled her daydreams. She hoped she wasn't being foolish.

"Same time tonight, at the park?" Rose let Satter take her hand.

"Afraid not, Rose. Pa needs me. He asked — well, I should say demanded — I help with harvesting peaches tonight. He's picking me up after I get off work. I'll spend the night there, and hitch a ride into town in the morning. It'll make for a long day." Satter brought her hand to his lips. "And, I'll miss you."

Swallowing her disappointment, Rose flicked an imaginary piece of lint from his shoulder. "Will you be free tomorrow evening? The Mission is playing its usual Friday night western. We'd need to get there early. You know how crazy it gets on China Night."

Rose was ashamed of her forwardness but hoped, with all her heart, Satter would say yes. He did. They made arrangements to meet outside the Hotel D' Hamburger at seven-fifteen.

Rose stopped by Mari's place on the way home. She wanted to invite her to dinner. With Papa still in the hospital, and Satter unavailable, she thought she'd make her friend a home-cooked meal.

No one answered her knock, so Rose tentatively tapped on Emma's door to see if Mari was working there.

"No, dearie, we just hired a new man to do odd jobs. She's around somewhere showing him the grounds. Would you like to come in and wait with us?"

Rose felt like a fly being invited into the parlor of a spider. She nervously shook her head and asked if she could find Mari and invite her to dinner.

"Don't be taking her away from her duties, dearie."

With a promise to be quick, Rose waved goodbye. It was the first time she'd ever ventured past Mari's door into the heart of Shantytown.

Five long bungalows sat like dominoes on Colorado Avenue. Each had three rooms occupied by Emma's "girls." Several trees shaded the dirt-packed alleyways, which were dappled with tufts of buffalo grass and dandelions. A stray dog crossed her path, his tail slunk between his hind legs. He relieved himself at the water pump.

Rose was thankful it was still too early to see anyone hanging about, advertising her wares. She wondered where all the cars were. At school, she'd overheard some boys bragging about how good the tips were on car-washing day. So where were they? Wandering down one alley, she finally caught sight of Mari's Packard parked next to several other vehicles. Hers looked pristine next to its weathered neighbors.

It was then she heard angry voices. Approaching them quietly, she peeked around the corner of a bungalow.

Mari stood with her back to Rose. Her posture was stiff and her arms jabbed the air in short bursts. She moved slightly, and Rose saw whom she was talking to. *Cecil.* What was he doing here?

Rose cupped her ear so she could hear better.

"Now, Mari, ya *jest* let me kiss ya. I ain't no rube, so stop playin' games!" Cecil pushed his hands through his hair and then began pacing back and forth. "I don't know if I'm comin' er goin' with ya. One time yer swell, an' the next ya cain't stand the sight o' me. Today, I git both! Don't ya know I adore ya?"

These last words were spoken as he grabbed Mari's shoulders. She jerked away from his grip. He stared at her, eyes sick with misery.

Mari's anger seemed to drain from her posture.

"Cecil," the woman's voice had the same quality one used to placate a child, "I ain't saying I'm not flattered, but Johnny's my sweetheart, right now."

"I moved from Oklahoma t' find ya, Mari. That should account fer somethin'."

"It does, Cecil."

Mari turned toward Rose, who pulled back behind her corner, but not before catching the woman roll her eyes skyward. When she peeked again, Mari was facing Cecil once more.

"And when I tire of Johnny, I'll let you call on me, again. You're too serious, Cecil, and right now, I just wanna have some fun." Mari put her hands behind her back and swiveled from side to side. Her voice became a purr. "You understand doncha? There's plenty of time to get serious. Okay?"

Cecil stuck his finger in Mari's face. "Okay, but ya jest 'member — one day yew'll be mine!" He turned on his heel and strode away.

Rose was about to call out to Mari, when she heard another voice speak up.

"Girl, have you gone and chased off our hired help, already?"

Rose saw Emma hobble from the next alley towards Mari. She didn't want to be caught spying, so she turned and ran back the way she came. Rose was leaning against Mari's doorjamb, when the two women finally appeared.

"Hey, kid, whatcha doing here?" Mari sounded weary.

"I wanted to ask you to dinner at my house tonight. Satter's got to help your pa after work. Can you come?"

Mari saw the pleading in Rose's eyes and nodded. "I'll be done here soon, and then I'll be over." She turned to Emma, who had been taking in the exchange with lively eyes.

"Pardon, Emma, but may I speak to the girl alone?"

Emma mumbled something under her breath as she hobbled toward her door.

Mari watched until the door was shut, then bent down to look Rose in the eye. "I don't wancha coming here again, you hear? This place ain't the best for an innocent like you. Now, I want your promise, this'll be the last time I'll see you in Shantytown."

"I promise, but what's wrong, Mari?" Rose noticed white lines of strain around her mouth. *Cecil has really upset my friend!*

"Nothing you need to worry your pretty head about. Now go on, scoot! I'll see you soon."

Rose looked over her shoulder when she reached the corner, and saw Mari watching her. She waved, and then hurried to Strange's Grocery.

Chapter Eight

*W*ith her arms full of ingredients for *Chicken Cacciatore,* Rose used her hip to hold the front door open. She'd been humming *Oh You Beautiful Doll,* and was about to break into song, when she saw her father.

Pale and thinner than he'd ever been, he sat at the table with his hands folded in front of him.

"P-Papa, what are you doing home?"

"I live here, or have you forgotten?"

Rose carried her groceries to the counter and laid them down. She took a deep breath before turning around.

"I meant, are you well enough to come home?"

"Well enough," her father said, starting to cough.

Immediately, Rose wanted to go to him, but was still crushed by the hurtful words he'd last spoken to her. She knew he could care less about her, so with grim resolution, she shredded her feelings of pity.

"Fine, since you are 'well enough,' we will be having a guest for dinner."

She pulled out a pot and pumped water into it. After placing it on the stove, she stoked the fire. She banged and smacked and thumped and slammed, not caring that she was making a lot of noise. If her father was bothered, he could just go back to the hospital where he was welcome!

"We need to talk."

"Pardon me, did you say something?" Rose held up the hammer she'd been using to tenderize the chicken breasts. She gave him a frosty look.

"You heard me, *girl*! I want to talk to you."

Papa's patrician nose lifted arrogantly, daring her to ignore his wishes. For a moment Rose wavered, but her fear passed into detached determination.

"I am too busy to talk with you right now. Why don't you wash up for dinner? Our guest will be here shortly." Rose folded her arms and cocked her head. "Oh, did I tell you about our guest? You may be acquainted with her. She's my new friend, Mari, and she lives a few blocks away. In *Shantytown*."

With satisfaction, Rose saw disbelief spread across her father's face.

"Mari helped me cut my hair. Do you like my new hairdo, Papa?" Smirking, Rose patted the soft waves.

Then she gasped. Her father was suddenly by her side, his fingers ensnared in her hair. He pulled hard, and she cried out in pain.

"You like to taunt your Papa, eh?" he said, spittle sprinkling her face. His eyes squinted into hard, black pebbles.

"Let go of me, Papa."

He pulled harder.

"Let go of me!" Rose balled up her fists. She'd smash her father's face in, if necessary.

"Bah!"

Rose's head snapped back, as he let go of her hair. They glared at one another, and then her father stalked toward his bedroom. With each step, energy shed off him like a discarded snakeskin. When he'd reached his doorway, he appeared half his size. The door closed with a click.

Good, Rose thought, as she rubbed her head.

She felt exhausted. Putting her hands to her hot cheeks, she realized that standing up for herself would take some getting used to. Shaking her head, she finished preparing dinner. She hoped her father would stay in his room when Mari came.

It occurred to Rose that it wasn't the best time to have her friend for dinner. She should have run over and cancelled as soon as she saw Papa was home. *Too late now.* Besides, how could she cancel? Mari made her promise never to step foot in Shantytown, again. Rose frowned. What in the world was going on with her friend?

Unfortunately, when Mari knocked, Rose's father opened his door and shuffled over to the table. Defiance smudged his eyes.

"Boy, what a day I've had!" Mari started through the door, then stopped short. "Why the long face, kid?"

With a jerk of her head, Rose indicated her father sitting at the table.

"Well, if it ain't your pa! Mari strode past Rose and stuck out her hand. "Last time we met, you was hanging over my shoulder like a sack of taters. Hope you're feeling better."

Papa ignored Mari's outstretched hand and said, "Why don't you go back where you belong, and leave my daughter alone?"

"I see we're gonna have some fun tonight, Rose." Mari winked over Papa's head, as if to say, "Don't worry, kid, this situation ain't too big for you and me to handle."

Rose, who had returned to the stove to begin serving, looked thoughtfully at Papa. He'd called her "daughter." It was the first time she'd ever heard him say that, and the coldness she felt for her father began to thaw. Maybe there was hope for them.

Rose retrieved the spare chair from her bedroom, then said, "Supper's ready. Why don't you take a seat, Mari?"

Her friend sat down opposite her father. Rose recognized the stubborn set to Mari's jaw, and felt a moment of trepidation. Mari smiled broadly at Papa. He did not return the smile.

It was going to be a very long meal, Rose decided.

Stiffly, grace was recited and then they began eating. The only sounds were forks and knives scraping on plates, the occasional wheeze from Papa's direction, and Mari's jaw clicking softly as she chewed. No one spoke.

Rose's gaze swung warily from her father to her friend, waiting for the fireworks to begin. She wasn't fooled by Mari's placid face. Her hazel eyes glimmered with calculated playfulness, a look that reminded Rose of a cat toying with a mouse. Poor Papa. He didn't know that he was about to be eaten alive.

Rose sighed, regretting her earlier bout of rebellion. She probably deserved what she got from Papa. After all, he'd just left his sickbed, and she had been disrespectful.

Without warning, she was flooded with a fierce love for these two people. Mari had become like a mother to her, and Papa — well, no matter what he did, she couldn't help but love him. She added another miracle to her prayer list, that Papa and Mari could accept one another. Being without either one would be unbearable.

The jarring silence was broken when Mari jabbed a piece of chicken with her fork and pointed it at Papa. "So," she smiled. "Rose tells me you beat her."

Both Papa and Rose blinked.

"Yep, I bet you think you're a big man, picking on your little girl."

"Mari?"

"Oh, it's all right, kid. I'm sure King Kong here don't mind everyone knowing he beats his daughter. Do you, *Papa?*"

"Don't call me *Papa*." Rose's father catapulted out of his seat like it had caught fire. His chair fell over backward.

Mari's gaze remained steady. "Rose shouldn't call you Papa, neither, since you don't treat her the way a papa oughta."

"Get out of my house!" Rose's father trembled as he stood in front of Mari. He pointed to the door.

Frozen in shock, Rose couldn't find her voice.

Undeterred, Mari cut a piece of chicken and put it in her mouth, chewing slowly. "Well now, I ain't finished with these fine vittles your dear daughter prepared. Ain't many young ladies know how to cook like her. Not that you'd appreciate that fact. But, I'm sure there's plenty of fellas in the world that would." Mari took her glass of wine and saluted Rose.

Papa grabbed the glass. Mari refused to let go. In the struggle, the stem broke and wine splashed down Papa's pants. He pulled back his fist, his intent plain.

Rose jumped up. "Papa, don't!"

"Touch me again, mister, and you're dead meat."

"Mari, what are you doing?" Rose wrestled herself between her father and her friend.

"Teaching this knucklehead a lesson. He's a bully, and I hate bullies!" Mari tried to reach past Rose.

Rose pushed on her friend's tense body. "He's sick, Mari," she pleaded. "I beg you, don't hurt him."

"You're darn tootin', he's sick. Sick in the head, if'n you ask me."

"And you're a filthy whore. You think that makes you better than me? Get out, I say!"

"Papa, it's not what you think. She just drives and keeps house for — "

"I don't care what she does, as long as *she gets out of my house!*"

Rose managed to break apart Mari and Papa. She picked up the fallen chair and held it out for her father.

"Papa," Rose ordered, "Sit down. Now! I will take care of this."

Her father flinched when Rose put her hand on his arm, but sat down on his chair. As she nudged Mari toward the door, he muttered curses under his breath. Rose thanked God they were in Italian, or her friend would have been right back in Papa's face.

Rose opened the screen door and pulled Mari onto the porch. She tried to make eye contact, but the woman kept glaring over Rose's shoulder.

"Mari." Rose shifted, so neither of them faced Papa. "Mari, I understand and appreciate what you're doing. And — thank you for wanting to protect me."

"Anything for you, kid." A small smile tugged at Mari's curled lip.

Rose rubbed her temples. "I can't stand to see the two people I love the most fighting. There's got to be a way for all of us to get along. And Mari," Rose touched her arm, "I'll need time to figure out how. Go home now, and I'll try to calm Papa down."

"I ain't leaving you with him! He'll hurt you, kid." Mari crushed Rose to her bosom. "Wait!" She pushed the girl an arm's length away. "Did you just say '*two* people I love'? Are you including me in that, Rose?"

"Yes, dear friend, I most certainly am. Now, go before any more damage is done." Rose gently pushed the woman down the stair.

Mari turned and said, "I'm rather fond of you, too."

Rose grinned. "I couldn't tell. Now shoo!"

The moon had begun its descent into the western hemisphere. Nick noticed he wasn't getting much work done, but his grandmother's story had mesmerized him.

Rose folded her hands together and rested her chin on them. "My heart was bursting with affection when I shut that door." She yawned delicately. "I wished I'd told Mari my feelings under different circumstances but, as it turned out, time had run out to say anything at all. I take comfort that, at least, it had been said . . ."

"Papa, Mari is my best friend. Why, she cares about me more than you ever did!"

Her father's eyes were cold with fury. Rose braced herself to be slapped silly for her impudence, already sure the pain would be worth it. She was surprised when he lowered his eyes. This gave her courage to continue. She squared her shoulders and declared, "I don't want you ever to talk to Mari like that, again!"

"People like her are dirt." Papa sniffed in disgust. "Whore!"

"She's *not* a whore! Mari cleans house for Emma and drives her around town." Rose crossed her arms. "And nothing more."

"Humph."

"Papa, what a hypocrite you are!" She bent close to her father's ear and whispered, "I know you visit Shantytown on occasion. Don't deny it; I've seen you."

Her father shot out of his chair, pushing Rose roughly. "I have my reasons for going there." He looked darkly toward the screen door. "And, I may have just found one more."

Chapter Nine

"**D**oc Sapero's in town."

Rose and Satter had ambled leisurely down Main Street and were stopped in front of the *Daily Sentinel* building. Satter was perusing the morning edition.

It was shortly after noon on Friday. The azure sky was spotted with popcorn clouds, and the air carried a slightly fruity fragrance from the ripe peach orchards. The ridges on the Bookcliff Mountains were unusually crisp and clear, as if the dusty summer air had been cleaned and polished.

Rose brushed at a swarm of gnats swimming around her face. As usual, she had dropped by the department store to join Satter for the noon meal. She hadn't been hungry, so she'd given the young man her basket, which held a stick of pepperoni and a chunk of bread. Rose had watched with amusement, as Satter first sunk his teeth into the spicy meat, then tore off a morsel of bread and stuffed it into his mouth. Smacking his lips after each bite, the basket had emptied within minutes.

"Who?"

"That specialist from Denver."

Rose raised her shoulders in ignorance.

Satter folded the newspaper so the advertisement was framed. "See, here. 'He has treated successfully disease of the eye, ear, nose and throat'."

Rose pulled the paper closer and squinted at the print. "It also says he takes care of deafness, toenails, adenoids, goiter and," Rose stumbled over the word, "catarrh."

Their heads together, Satter mumbled, "Whatever *that* is. Hey," he tapped the paper, "consultation and examination are free! I should tell Mari 'bout this. Her Teddy stubbed his toe, again. I bet the good Doc could help. He's just across from her place, at the LaCourt Hotel."

"I wished I'd known. I could have told her when she came to supper yesterday." Rose bowed her head. "I guess we didn't have much time for talk. She, um, had to leave rather hurriedly."

"It didn't happen 'til last evening, anyway. She was out to the farm after supper. For some reason, she had a hankering to play with Teddy." Satter tucked the folded paper under one arm and held out an elbow for Rose. "He stubbed his toe when they was playing hide-and-go-seek."

"Did Mari tell you about Papa?"

"She made mention of some sorta stink." He glanced sideways at Rose. "Everything okey-dokey?"

"It will be, someday." Rose slipped her arm through Satter's and started walking fast. "Come on, I don't want to waste any more time talking about it."

When they'd reached the entrance to J.C. Penney's, the conversation had come around to Mari again.

"Are you going to tell her about Dr. Sapero? I'd do it, but she made me promise never to go to Shantytown, again."

Satter pulled out his pocket watch, checked the time, and then snapped it shut. "I could run over right now and fill her in. How 'bout I invite her and Johnny to the movies with us, too?"

"That sounds nifty." Rose glanced down at her sneakers, and noticed her right toe was scuffed. She hid it behind her left heel. "Satter, did Mari happen to mention why she didn't want me hanging around Shantytown? Did I do something wrong?"

"Walk with me a ways, Rose." Satter guided the girl westward on Main. "S'matter of fact, she did mention something peculiar to Pa. He made light of it, but I saw the concern on Mari's face." They'd reached the Hotel D'Hamburger, across from the LaCourt Hotel. "I didn't hear all of what she said, but I did hear the words, 'white slavery' and 'Emma'."

"White slavery?"

"Yep."

"What's that?"

"I don't reckon a good Italian girl would be familiar with such things, and I ain't saying I know much about it, neither," Satter's color had risen, "but I heard there's a ring near the border of Utah that buys young girls."

"*Buys* girls?"

Satter cleared his throat, embarrassed to be discussing this with Rose. "Well, um, for pleasure, if you know what I mean."

"My goodness!" Rose's hands flew to her cheeks. Flustered, she quickly looked down at the ground.

Satter lifted her chin gently, and kissed the end of her nose. "I'm sorry. I shoulda known better than to expose you to the seedy side of life."

Rose's toes were tingling from the kiss, but she looked defiantly at him. "I know more about that side of life than you realize! My own papa — " She wanted to clap her hand to her mouth. She wasn't ready to share that secret, even with Satter. "Is Mari in any danger?"

Satter saw her concern and scooped her into an embrace. "Now, only a fool would mess with Mari. She'd hogtie him and serve him to the buzzards." He looked past the LaCourt Hotel to the corner of Shantytown. "'Haps she's concerned for you. She's mighty fond of you, Rose, and I know she'd do anything to protect you from harm." His eyes filled with affection. "That makes two of us."

Rose felt light-headed. Pushing Satter toward the street, she said, "I don't need protecting, but thank you anyway. Now, you better be going. You don't want to be late for work."

Satter saluted. "Yes, ma'am. See you right here, seven-fifteen sharp."

"I'm sorry I'm late, Satter. Mrs. Baldino asked me to watch her youngest, who's feeling poorly, while she went to the grocer. Then, Rollie spit up on my dress, so I had to change. And just as I was leaving, Papa came home! He never comes home on Friday, at least not until late. I had to crawl out my bedroom window to come here."

Satter had been sitting on the curb in front of the Hotel D'Hamburger. When Rose appeared, he stood and leisurely stretched. She admired him, as his ample muscles became defined. The sight made her breathless.

"That's okay, Rose," the young man drawled, tucking his shirt and straightening his suspenders with a satisfied snap.

With an effort, she tore her eyes away, acutely aware of the pleasing warmth seeping down toward her knees. Rose looked around. Mari was nowhere in sight, and she needed a distraction!

"She won't be joining us tonight," Satter explained. "Darned — I mean, derned if Mari didn't take off in a car ten minutes ago with a coupla fellas." He shook his head in disgust. "She told me to tell Johnny she was sick and had to go home. I don't know what gets into that girl sometimes."

Rose couldn't hide her disappointment. She'd wanted to tell Mari how she'd stood up to Papa. "Where'd she go?"

Satter shrugged. "I been into the restaurant several times to tell Johnny, but Olive won't let me disturb him until his shift is over. I don't want to leave him in the lurch, so I hope you don't mind if we wait."

He sat down again and patted the curb next to him. Rose joined him, and welcomed the arm that drew her close.

"Make a wish, Rose."

Rose looked heavenward. Clouds hunkered together like unfurled sailboats racing across a deep blue sea. The first star had just emerged in their wake. She knew what she wanted to wish, but did she dare? She looked at Satter out of the corner of her eye. He was so handsome. And he treated her like a queen. Who wouldn't want to be married to such a man?

"There's that look in your eyes, again."

Rose was startled. He couldn't have read her mind, could he? She forced her paralyzed mouth to move. "Wh-what look?"

"The one that makes my innards melt into a puddle of mush." Satter shifted to face her, folding her hands in his. "The one that makes me want to take care of you forever."

A pulse began beating furiously in her throat, nearly strangling her. Every night, since their first date, she'd imagined hearing words like this from him.

"Satter?"

His lips muffled the joy in her voice.

Rose could hardly keep her mind on the action exploding on the big screen. They had skipped the western and were seated in the balcony of the Avalon Theater, watching a movie about an elephant boy and his adventures in Africa. Satter sat on one side of her. Johnny, who to Rose's chagrin, had opted to join them, sat on the other. A box of buttered popcorn rested on her lap, available for any of their hands to reach. Johnny dipped into the box unceasingly, his constant crunching aggravating her left ear. Finally, Rose slipped the popcorn onto his lap and snuggled closer to Satter. She was too happy to snack, anyway.

The darkness was filled with the strident sounds of elephants stampeding amidst the cacophonous noise of jungles. Rose should have been thrilled with the exciting story, but all she could concentrate on was Satter's presence next to her. His arm had been draped over her shoulder since the moment they'd sat down and, every few minutes, he bestowed a proprietary smile on her.

The audience collectively gasped and shuddered, as an enraged elephant reared onto its hind legs, threatening to crush a poor village boy. Rose took this opportunity to snuggle closer to her companion, shivering in feigned mortal fear. She pressed her head against his shoulder. A small contented sigh escaped, but was engulfed in the wave of relief that swept over the theater, as the child miraculously avoided injury.

When the audience poured out the exits into the breezy evening, Satter once again apologized to Johnny for Mari's absence. He felt bad lying about his sister's whereabouts and planned to give her an earful the next day.

"Heck, don't make no never mind to me." Johnny's ears danced in time with his words. Frown lines momentarily bracketed his mouth, but then he smiled, displaying a broad band of white teeth. "You know how these womenfolk can be. 'Specially at certain times o' the month."

Satter's face flushed. "Well now," he cleared his throat, "volumes could be written about what I don't know concerning the mysterious workings of womenfolk." He avoided Rose's merry eyes.

"Johnny," he held out his hand, "you have a nice evenin'. I'm gonna walk my gal home, and then hike out to Pa's farm for the night."

The young men shook hands, and then Johnny trotted eastward. Satter and Rose watched long after the young man's lanky form had melted into the shadows, as if afraid to finally face each other alone. The crowd had fractured into smaller groups, snippets of conversations flurrying in the breeze. A web of silence surrounded the couple.

Rose found the courage to begin. "I'm having a wonderful time." She batted her eyelashes the way she'd seen Mari do to Johnny. "And, I'm certainly not ready to be walked home, yet."

"Don't do that."

"Wh-what?" Rose felt her stomach convulse at Satter's stern face. *Have I messed up our romance, already?*

"That thing you just did with your lashes." His eyes swept the crowd, before he pulled Rose around the corner of the theater for privacy. "It reminds me of how Mari acts around her fellas."

"I'm sorry. It's just — I like Mari and want to be like her."

"There's lots of things I like about my sister, but how she handles romance makes my blood boil." He ran his finger gently down Rose's cheek. "You don't need to do those kinds of things, 'specially with me, Rose. You're the gal of my dreams, and I like you just the way you are."

"Okay." Her voice squeaked, and Satter laughed.

"Now, don't get all het up, beautiful." He wrapped his arms around Rose. She relaxed, and then giggled as she heard his stomach rumble loudly.

"Hungry?"

"I *am* a bit." Satter grinned. "After all, that boy ate the whole box of popcorn!"

They wandered down Main Street, passing a patrolman who was dragging a disheveled man out of the gutter. In warm months, hobos littered Grand Junction's parks, alleys and streets like flotsam after a flood.

Occasionally, Rose ran into a group of them near the railroad tracks, predictably eating out of cans of beans they'd warmed over a makeshift fire. She knew when the frigid winter fronts started to roll in, the town would clear, as the homeless hopped the trains and headed westward toward Arizona and California.

Rose wasn't afraid of these men but, rather, felt sorry for them. It bothered her that work was still hard to find. After all, nearly a decade had passed since the collapse of Wall Street and the ensuing national economic depression.

As the couple watched, the policeman jerked the man to a sitting position and handcuffed him before tossing him in the back of a paddy wagon with a sickening thud. A surge of indignation rose in her throat, but Satter waylaid it by pushing her past the scene.

"It doesn't pay to rile the police, Rose. He's just doing his duty."

"That isn't any way to treat another human being. The poor man may be down on his luck right now, but God loves him — even in the gutter. Treating him like an animal won't change his situation."

"There'll always be downtrodden and misunderstood folks, Rose. Better accept the truth of it."

"Humph. That doesn't mean I have to like it."

They came to the entrance of the Silver Moon Café. Inside, it looked very much like the first time the two ate together. Even that goofy young man, Everett, sat at his table with his nose in a book, as if he'd never left. Rose wondered if he was still reading *20,000 Leagues Under The Sea.*

Soon, the warmth and aromas and comfortable murmur of the café soothed Rose. Sitting next to Satter, she held his hand under the table, while they waited for a roast beef supper for him and a chocolate malted for her. Enjoying a companionable silence, they watched the patrons.

"That man looks familiar."

Rose lifted her chin toward an older gentleman in a pinstriped suit, dark waistcoat and silk tie. He stood above six other well-dressed men seated at a large table. Rose thought, with amusement, he must be part Italian, for he spoke with expressive gestures and copious words. The occupants of the table listened with avid eyes, as he told some humorous story. Frequent shouts of laughter rifted through the savory air.

"That's Sheriff Lumley. A frequent customer at the store." Satter rearranged his features into beaming bonhomie and lifted an imaginary hat in greeting.

His antics perfectly characterized the shoulder-clapping man who had approached Satter's boss, Mr. Class, when Rose couldn't find Satter. She giggled.

"That's pretty good!"

Satter inclined his head in mock pride. "I should go into politics, eh?" He started shaking imaginary hands and passing out toothy smiles.

Rose examined his face, as he mimicked the mannerisms of the sheriff. How she loved Satter! She saw earnestness cast in the line of his jaw, honesty in the sensuous set of his lips, and compassion and kindness reflected in his vivid blue eyes.

"You joke," Rose said, as the waitress placed their orders in front of them, "but the world could use a man like you in politics."

Little Italy's homes were settled and its occupants slumbering, when Satter drew Rose up on her porch for a goodnight kiss. After eating, they'd strolled the streets talking until nearly every light was extinguished and Rose couldn't stifle her yawning. Satter's kiss, sweet and lingering, ignited her senses briefly, but she was grateful to climb into bed and collapse into swift sleep.

Sometime in the night, Rose sat up with a start, as shrieks from a nearby cat fight slivered her subconscious. Irritated, she nestled into the warm indentation in her pillow again and waited for quiet to return. But sleep eluded her. The house was too quiet. No snoring. *Surely Papa is asleep by now.* With visions of her father, once again, lying in his vomit, she donned her cotton robe and tiptoed out of her bedroom. The clock above the stove said four forty-five.

"Papa?" She tapped on his door and listened for slumbering sounds with her ear close to the wood. It was as quiet as a tomb on the other side. With a sense of foreboding, she turned the knob and inched the door open. Her father's bedcovers were crisp and untouched.

"Papa!" *Where could he be?*

A quick perusal told Rose her father was nowhere in the house. She checked around the yard, ending up at the root cellar. Yanking the heavy door up, she recoiled when a startled bull snake slithered down the stone steps and disappeared into the inky pool at the bottom. No one lay crumpled in a heap, so she let the door drop shut.

Now what?

Worry whipped through her mind. A dozen dreadful scenarios could explain Papa's absence. Drunk or not, he should have been home long before now. Maybe he'd had a relapse of pneumonia and was lying dead somewhere! *Now, don't be melodramatic, girl! There's probably a good explanation.* She thought of waking Mrs. Baldino, but remembered little Rollie had been sick. She didn't need to be woken and worried over what may turn out to be a wild goose chase.

Mari! Wryly, Rose acknowledged that her unpretentious friend had become somewhat of a savior to her. Whenever she was in trouble, Mari saved the day.

Not bothering to change into street clothes, she wrapped her robe tight against the cool morning breeze and ran toward Shantytown. Just as she rounded the corner of the New World Café, she pulled back quickly.

Her father was slipping out of Shantytown's shadows in the direction of home. Though very much alive, his stealthy, liquid movements led Rose to believe something was very wrong. A recent scene flashed through her memory, of Papa's fierce words directed at Mari. Pin prickles of fear shot painfully through her limbs, as she realized Mari might be in danger.

Lord, let me be wrong!

Rose waited until her father was out of sight, then she stumbled toward Shantytown, her feet heavy as if slogging through mud.

Chapter Ten

*T*he alley was dark; elm trees blotted out the first fragments of dawn. Rose's pounding heart threatened to close off her windpipe, and her hands were drenched. She wiped her palms on her robe and forced yet another step. Somewhere near, a motor started up, its whine diminishing as the vehicle sped down the street and out of earshot. Rose stopped. What if she encountered a Shantytown patron leaving?

Impatiently, she brushed away the thought. *You have bigger things to worry about, girl!* She stared through the shadowy veil, barely able to make out the outline of her friend's bungalow.

Suddenly, a shower of light burst through Mari's window, splashing onto the dirt below and sharply defining Emma Splott's house across the alley.

What in blue blazes? It looked like something had exploded inside, but no percussion followed.

Just as quickly as it appeared, the light was gone.

Rose was momentarily blinded by the sudden darkness. Motionless, she waited for her night vision — and courage — to return. She seriously considered turning around and running back to bed. Mari would be all right. Even if Papa had done something bad, she'd come out on top, just like Satter said. Snuggled under her bedcovers, Rose could pretend that Papa had come home, drunk as usual, and all was right with the world. Her shoulders sagged. That was the trouble. It would only be pretend, for Rose had a sinking feeling that when she knocked on Mari's door, nothing would ever be right again.

Come on, kid, quit feeling sorry for yourself. Where's your moxie?

"Somehow, that girl had wormed her way, not only into my heart, but my mind." Rose glanced at the lightening sky and clicked off the flashlight. Dropping it on the ground, she said, "Even in my subconscious, she encouraged me to face life with courage, to embrace even the frightening parts." Rose watched her grandson tamp down the spongy squares of grass he'd dug up. With the toe of her shoe, she nudged a small, forgotten clump toward him. "I wonder if she'll ever know how her wisdom changed me."

Nicky, who'd been thinking the same thing about his grandmother, said, "She surely does now, Nonna."

Rose wasn't ready for what was on the other side of that door. Grave concern for Mari overcame her fear, and she slowly approached the entry. It was unlocked, so she tapped on the inner door and listened. There was no answer. Rose took a deep breath and flung the door open.

This time, the room was not empty. Mari lay, half-naked, across her bed, an arm flung over her head. She was unnaturally still.

"Oh, Papa, what have you done?" Rose was beside her friend in an instant. "Mari! Wake up!" She shook her arm, tears wetting her cheeks.

For some reason, Mari's bloomers had been soaked in water and were scrunched at the base of her jaw line. *Why did he do that?* When Rose withdrew the garment, she gasped. Bruises in the shape of fingertips formed an ugly necklace against her ivory skin.

"No!"

Was Mari still breathing? Wildly, Rose looked around for a mirror. Spotting the little one hanging on the wall above the chair, she dashed over and pulled it from its nail. Her fingers were clumsy and she lost her grip. The mirror cartwheeled down her leg. Lunging for it, she cried with relief when it bounced onto the chair. The apron, which lay bunched on the seat, had cushioned its fall.

Just then, Mari moaned. It was a tiny sound, yet it filled Rose with staggering joy.

"Dearest Mari, you're alive!"

She picked her way across the bed, being careful, this time, not to jostle her friend. Rose faltered when she saw the bruises had darkened, and replaced the damp bloomers, hoping the coolness would stop their progress. She anxiously waited for another moan, or any sign the woman was still among the living.

"Lord, help my friend!" She gently took Mari's hand and kissed it. "I beg You, tell me what to do."

Satter.

Yes, of course! Satter would know what to do. Didn't he say he was staying the night at his folks'? Rose wiped her tears and cried, "Hold on, Mari! Please."

She thanked God that Mari had taught her to drive and looked around for the Packard's keys. She found them hidden under Teddy's picture, which had tumbled from its usual place. Curiously, several of Mari's drawers were pulled halfway out and her clothes jumbled, as if someone had rifled through them. With no time to wonder, she headed for the door. Just as she pulled it open, she became aware of the fragrance of roses. She hadn't noticed before, but it filled the room and was sweeter than anything she'd ever smelled.

Rose dredged her memory for details of where Satter's folks lived. At least she knew it was out Fruitvale way. As she drove, other bits of information shuffled to the surface. *Look for Eleanor Roosevelt in britches. And didn't they live in a converted train car?*

Sure such a unique place would stick out plainly, Rose drove confidently up and down farm roads. The sun had fully breached the Grand Mesa's horizon when Rose finally gave up. She pounded the steering wheel in frustration. Fighting down the urge to scream, she sped back to town. She'd have to find someone else to help Mari.

When she arrived, Shantytown was a pandemonium of people. A police car and medical examiner's wagon blocked the alleyway, while a large group of women, in various degrees of undress, huddled together against the chill morning. All were stretching their necks to watch the goings on. Rose was relieved help had arrived and parked the car down the street.

"No admittance," a tall man in uniform commanded, when Rose had pushed her way through the milling women. His raisin eyes dismissed her, passing over her head to scan the crowd for more important miscreants.

"Please, Officer!" Rose tugged at his sleeve. "Is Mari all right? I must know! She's my friend and when I found her earlier, she was badly hurt."

"What do you mean, you found her? *She,*" he jerked his head toward the alley, "found her. Now run along, kid. This ain't no place for you." He made shooing motions with his hands, and then shouted to his left, "Hey, toots, back behind the vehicle!"

The officer's attention was drawn away, so Rose peeked under the man's elbow at the milieu in the alley. She saw Emma Splott gesturing wildly while talking to Sheriff Lumley. He scribbled rapidly in a small tablet. His normally jovial face was serious. Just then, a hush fell over the area, as two men carried out a sheet-draped stretcher and slid it into the interior of the ME's wagon. The breeze flipped up the corner of the sheet, revealing Mari's face. To Rose, it looked like a wax mask, devoid of any familiar animation. A collective "Oh!" ricocheted around her.

"No!" Rose tried to shimmy past the officer who, once again, blocked her way.

"Hey, where do you think you're going?"

"Mari can't be dead, I tell you. She's — "

"Didn't I tell you to scram? Now git!" The policeman grabbed Rose's neck and roughly escorted her out of Shantytown. Rude remarks were tossed his way, as he cut through the throng.

"Hey, that ain't no way t' treat a baby!"

Rose tried not to stare at the woman, whose rouged smile streaked across both cheeks.

"Whatsa matta wit' ya, ya big palooka?" another woman hollered, her voice slurred.

"Mind your own potatoes," the man shot back. When they'd reached the alley, he pushed the girl away from him. With arms akimbo, he sternly watched, as Rose reluctantly turned toward Little Italy.

The heartache she felt was beyond description. It was as if her spirit had been ripped from her body and she was forced to exist in the remaining shell. Rose stared helplessly around.

She didn't want to go home. Home was where her Papa was. *Her* Papa, *Mari's* murderer. Fear charged through her. She had to find Satter. He'd know what to do about Papa. Wait! Her frantic thoughts slammed into one another as she realized she couldn't turn her father over to the authorities. That just wasn't done in Little Italy. Besides, maybe, she was wrong. Maybe, he didn't do it. He was just in the wrong place at the wrong time. Rose cried in relief. Papa couldn't be a murderer! Could he?

It took every bit of bravery to sneak into the house and change her clothes. It helped, knowing she must tell Satter the terrible news, and quickly. He'd be devastated over Mari's death, but it would be better to hear it from Rose than some policeman.

"Mr. Class, I need to speak with Satter. It's very important." Rose looked imploring at the man.

"He's with Mrs. Newman, young lady, and knowing her propensity for shoes," Satter's boss preened an eyebrow, "he'll be with her for quite awhile." He steered Rose toward the front of the store. "Perhaps, you'd like to come back at noontime, yes?"

Rose would not be put off. "Sir, his sister died this morning." She looked pointedly at the older man. "Killed. Don't you think a death is more important than some crummy shoe sale?" Her voice had risen to a hysterical screech.

"Oh, my!" The man turned on his heel and strode over to Satter. He leaned down and whispered something in the boy's ear, and then seated himself on the deserted stool.

Satter's blue eyes drank Rose in like she was a tall glass of lemonade on a lazy summer afternoon. They also held a hint of surprise at her unscheduled visit. She felt a pang of remorse that instead of responding to his love, she had to shatter his world. Avoiding his eyes, she waved him toward the curtained stock room. His happy surprise changed to confusion.

She cleared her throat several times before she was able to speak without her voice catching. "Satter — "

"Rose, what's wrong?" The young man drew the girl into his arms. "Whatever it is, we can handle it together. You and me." Still holding her close, he lifted her chin so her face was raised, and brushed her lips with his. "Tell me."

Tears splashed down Rose's cheeks, as she spoke the words she dreaded saying. "It's Mari, Satter. She's dead!"

"What?"

"Murdered. In her own bed."

Satter held Rose at arm's length. "T'aint funny, McGee!"

Rose's face crumpled. "I found her."

He took her by the arm and they advanced on Mr. Class. "I have to leave, sir." As they strode out the door, Satter grimly looked at Rose.

"Tell me everything."

"Now, don't get yourself in a lather, sonny."

Rose held tightly to Satter's hand, trying to keep it from connecting with the man's jaw. Detective Keith Jordan calmly stood his ground, as Satter sputtered his indignation just inches from the man's face.

"You ain't talking to no rube, mister! I want to see my sister, or else!"

"Satter, maybe we — "

The young man pulled his hand out of Rose's grasp and stabbed a finger in the detective's chest. Satter opened his mouth as if to object, but before he could say anything, the detective grabbed his arm and twisted it, immobilizing him. Anguish infused Satter's face.

"Shove in your clutch and seat yourselves yonder. I'll see what I can find out." He pushed Satter, none too gently, in the direction of a wooden bench located by the far wall of the police station.

Satter rubbed his arm, while Rose sat next to him. She watched the detective saunter into a nearby office. Through the doorway, she saw him perch on the corner of a metal desk and speak to the man sitting there. Both gave the couple a measured look, before the man at the desk nodded. The detective touched his brow in a cocky salute and then approached the couple.

"Seems the boss has a soft side," he drawled, when he was within earshot. He veered toward the entrance, where a hat stand stood sentinel. Donning a fedora, he pulled open the door. "Come on, then," he tossed over his shoulder.

When Rose and Satter had climbed into the back of the police car, the detective slammed their door and scooted behind the steering wheel. The ride to Crown Funeral Home was short, with a charged quietness. The only interruption was their driver's occasional tuneless whistling. Every once in a while, he'd look at them in the rear view mirror.

"I feel like a criminal," whispered Rose.

Satter kept his eyes locked on the back of the detective's head. "This better not be phonus bolonus." His words were squeezed through clenched teeth.

"Shh." Rose looked anxiously at Detective Jordan. "Let's not make needless enemies." She slipped her hand through his arm and tentatively leaned her head on his shoulder. Since she'd told Satter about Mari's death, he'd not acted like himself.

This frightened her. In one night, it seemed as if she'd lost nearly everyone precious to her. How could she go on if she lost Satter, too? She began to tremble uncontrollably. Rose was surprised when Satter reached over and patted her hand. She looked at him gratefully.

He must never know about Papa!

The interior of the funeral home was dark and heavy with the smell of pine and formaldehyde. Rose recoiled from the sense of death that imbued the atmosphere.

"Bet you didn't know these fancy pine boxes are made by Bannister's Furniture, did you?"

"No, and I ain't interested, neither," Satter hissed at the detective. He ignored Rose's nervous tugging. "Now, where's my sister?"

At that moment, a man emerged from a back room and shuffled toward another door. He paid no attention to the waiting group. Satter strode after the man.

"Where's Mari?"

His shirtsleeves were scrunched up to his elbows and his apron, splotched with mysterious stains, covered him to his knees. Blond hair jutted out in different directions, topping a ruddy face. The rectangle reading glasses balanced on the tip of his bulbous nose underlined his look of distraction. It seemed a great effort for the man to direct his pale gaze at Satter.

"Hmm? What is it, boy?"

"No point in asking him anything." A woman had appeared from behind a curtained arch. "My husband is the most absent-minded creature on God's good earth." The woman's thin lips stretched into a generous smile to show this didn't bother her in the least. "I'm Mrs. Crown, the Coroner."

She glided toward them. Barely reaching Rose's shoulder, she was as round as she was tall. Her green eyes were youthful and full of compassion, as she examined first Rose's face, then Satter's. She took his hand and sandwiched it between hers. Strong, sinewy fingers caressed his skin.

"You've lost someone."

Rose saw tears form and spill down his cheeks.

"Yes, ma'am, I most certainly have. Is my sister here? Her name is Marietta Monroe."

With a start, Rose realized she'd never known what her friend's surname was.

"Ah, indeed, she is." She glanced at the closed door her husband had disappeared through. "Doctors Monro and Jaros are still with her."

"I want to see her."

"You must wait, I'm afraid." Mrs. Crown, with a kindly gesture, indicated they should sit on the nearby chairs.

"Damn it, I won't! I'm through sitting!" Satter pushed past the woman, flung open the door, and stopped as if he'd struck an invisible wall. A look of horror crossed his face. Rose rushed to his side and cried out when she saw Mari, lying on a long, metal slab.

"Dear Lord," she gasped.

Dr. Monro stepped in front of the body, while the other doctor quickly drew a sheet over Mari. Mr. Crown sat at a desk, mumbling over paperwork and oblivious to the drama going on around him.

"What's the meaning of this?" Dr. Monro demanded, as he advanced on them. He looked at Rose. "Young lady, what are you doing here?"

Rose, who had covered her mouth with her hand, stared at the doctor, but couldn't make a sound. Though the doctor held out a restraining arm, she followed Satter over to the body. He lifted the corner of the sheet to reveal his sister's face. Mari could have been sleeping, but for tiny blood dots around her eyes, and the immediate awareness that life had seeped from her features. Rose avoided looking farther down, knowing that bruises, caused by her own father's fingers, encircled Mari's neck. She turned into Dr. Monro's embrace, shoulders shaking as she sobbed.

"Sonny, wait — "

Rose looked up and saw Satter dart past the detective and out the door. She rubbed at her tears and ran after Satter, catching him in the sunshine. He was bent over taking deep breaths.

"Satter, are you all right?"

The young man stood up, his face mottled with rage. Suddenly afraid, she withdrew her hand.

"I'm gonna get who did this!" He glared at the funeral home, then turned on his heel and ran down the street.

Chapter Eleven

"*I can understand his feelings, Nonna. His need for revenge.*"

"*I know, Nicky. When Katharine was killed by that drunk driver, you were inconsolable. We all were. So many hopes and dreams died because of a selfish, senseless act. But, even the trial and sentencing didn't bring you closure. Your rage still festered, and,*" Rose touched her grandson's shoulder, "*I have become afraid for you. That is the other reason we are here.*"

Rose stood rooted to the pavement. A *Good Humor* truck passed through a nearby neighborhood, and she listened to its melodious strains. She imagined the gaggle of children that would clamor around the truck when it stopped, mouths watering for a chocolate-covered vanilla ice cream bar. When Rose was young, the rare treat had always melted her girlhood anxieties. If only she were still a child, for no amount of ice cream could melt away her present nightmare.

Papa remained absent all day, and Rose assumed he'd gone to the railroad yard. But, he still hadn't appeared by bedtime, and the house echoed with loneliness and worry. Rose eagerly sought the oblivion of sleep.

It wasn't until she'd fallen woodenly into bed, that Rose remembered Mari's Packard. She threw back the covers and fished in the pocket of her dress until her fingers closed around the key. Tomorrow, she must find Satter and give him the car. Maybe, it would offer him some comfort.

In the dark, sleep evaded Rose. She felt hollow and lost. She squeezed her eyelids tight, but to no avail.

Fears for her father tossed uneasily around her mind. Why couldn't he have just left well enough alone? Gotten drunk, as usual, and drowned his anger toward Mari. *I hate him!* She thought of turning him in to the police, and shuddered. As horrified as she was with him, she couldn't possible betray her own blood.

Restless, she remembered her mother's journal and, once again, left the cocoon of her covers. She padded into her father's room and lifted the mattress. The book wasn't there. After a moment of frantic searching, she discovered it tucked under her father's pillow. It's weight brought instant solace.

Back in bed, she willed herself to think of good things, but Mari's vacant face clouded her mind.

Until that morning, death had never frightened Rose. She'd often prayed to die young. To die meant she'd finally be with her mother.

When she was thirteen, she'd had a dream so real, she'd felt sure she'd entered the Promised Land. The crystal blue sky had needed no sun to illuminate the subtle hills of brilliant emerald or the flowering brook, where, with other children, she'd played with Jesus. Feelings of love and peace and joy had dissolved into deep disappointment, when she'd awoken to Papa's snoring.

Until today, death had held the promise of happiness, but after seeing Mari's body, Rose realized death was a wretched process — an agonizing odyssey for the soul rent from its familiar home. With a sick feeling, she sent up a quick plea to die peacefully in her sleep at a ripe old age. She no longer wanted to die young, even knowing that after the painful journey, she would find happiness. And Mama.

But, would she find Mari? Would she be allowed to enter heaven when, on earth, she hadn't believed? And, what of Papa? Murderers were definitely not allowed in! These terrible questions brought a cascade of tears. Clutching her mother's journal to her breast, she pulled the sheet over her head and wept into her pillow.

The next morning, after a fitful night, Rose dressed for church. She really didn't want to go. To meet people and pretend all was fine seemed daunting, and the prospect made her stomach hurt. But, being alone with her fears was more unsettling.

A knock sounded at the door, and she froze. Opening it an inch, she peeked through the crack. A man, dressed in work clothes, stood there with an apologetic look on his face.

"May I help you?"

"Missa Rose? I'ma Tony Serra, ana I work wit' you father. I'm asorry to asaya it, but Sante, he agot turrible sicka yestaday. Da railroad, deya take him to de hospital. Looks alike de pneumonia, agin."

"He what?" She flung open the door. "He's at St. Mary's?"

"No, amissa, de railroad, dey atake dey ill ana hurta to de Salida hospital. I shoulda stopped bya lasta night, but mya dear Raffelina's time had acome. Li'l Amore was aborn only an hour ago." He yawned hugely. "Wella, I abetter be to aworka, now."

"Mr. Serra, thank you for taking time to call. I-I hope little Amore and your wife are well." She closed the door and leaned against it. So. Looking wearily around her, she decided she couldn't stare at the walls another second. Grabbing a wrap, she escaped to her neighbor's house.

In Italian families, everyone has a role. Husbands are the providers, wives and mothers are the hearts of their families, and children the hands and feet. The system worked well and balanced the whole community. At the moment, Rose needed some semblance of balance.

When she knocked, Mrs. Baldino's third son, Joseph, answered the door. Amiable activity went on behind him, as numerous children scurried about helping with breakfast. Joseph let Rose in. Mrs. Baldino, dressed in her Sunday best, called out orders from the stove. She watched, as the woman lifted the lid of the large pot simmering on the back burner and gave the ingredients a swift stir.

Appreciatively, Rose sniffed the aroma of vegetable beef soup.

Like most Italian homes, it was small with little decoration, but carried a warm and welcoming air. Rose felt her tension loosen. She sat on a kitchen chair and pulled Joseph upon her lap, absorbing the comfortable sounds of life being lived well.

"Rose, dear, I read about your friend. My sincere condolences. How strange that she should be," she whispered over little Joseph's head, "strangled by an apron string."

Rose lowered her voice, too. "I don't know anything about that. When I found her, there was no apron string around her neck. Just a lot of bruises."

She hated that Mari's death would be the talk of the town and, as usual, all sorts of misinformation would get mixed into the gossip.

"When *you* found her? Child, there's nothing about that in the newspaper. It says the old woman, the madam of that God-forsaken place, found her."

"Well, the paper is wrong. Emma found her later. I found her first." Disgruntled, she said, "I don't really want to talk about this." She let Joseph slide to his feet. "Do I smell bacon?"

She helped clear away breakfast, and, after Mrs. Baldino sent the children to scrub up for Mass, they sat down at the table. The older woman began threading a darning needle. Rose handed her a pair of scissors at her elbow and told the woman about Papa's falling ill again.

"That's a shame, Rose. I'll look in on you while he's recovering in Salida."

"It's not necessary, ma'am. I'm able to take care of myself. It's just — "

"What is it?" Mrs. Baldino's needle paused in midair.

"I'm not sure I can live with Papa, anymore."

The sock she was darning dropped to her lap, as Mrs. Baldino struggled to cover her dismay. "It's bound to get better, Rose."

"I've lost all hope." The girl leaned forward. "I've been waiting for a miracle all of my life, but God has not seen fit to grant it, ma'am. Maybe, I haven't been good enough, or I've sinned too much, or didn't say enough prayers. But, the fact is, Papa will never love me."

Mrs. Baldino took up her sewing, again. "He used to give Sunday evening concerts, you know."

"What?" Rose sat up straight.

Mrs. Baldino tilted her head in amusement. "When the railroad was being laid in eastern Utah." She snipped the thread after tying a knot. "Sante had a beautiful tenor voice, and after supper, he'd gather the *paesani* at the riverbank and train them. Every Sunday night, he'd give a concert where the men would sing folk songs from the Old Country. My Frank said there was never a dry eye. Sante could have joined the opera, if he'd wanted." She shook her head, sadly. "When Maria Rosa died, so did his remarkable talent."

As usual, Rose sat next to the aisle. Father Nick's sermon did nothing to soothe her. Maybe she was tired, or, maybe her fears had begun to jade her faith. The Scripture the priest quoted from was Psalm 37; *"Fret not thyself because of evildoers, neither be thou envious against the workers of iniquity. They shall soon be cut down like the grass and wither as the green herb."* This only helped increase her anxiety.

Even if Papa was the greatest of evildoers, she trembled at the thought of him being, "cut down like the grass." It was such a hopeless and permanent solution. Forgiveness seemed a better way to answer evil.

While mulling over this, Holy Communion began. When it was her pew's turn to go forward, the usher tapped her shoulder. Rose started to stand up, but remembered she'd missed confession. She shook her head slightly at the man before swiftly reseating herself. His dour look skewered her to the pew. Embarrassed, she was sure it was obvious to everyone that she was a pathetic person, lacking the appropriate character and spiritual responsibility to bear the name of Christian.

If only they knew how right they were. Long before Mass had concluded, Rose had snuck out.

It was unnerving standing in the sunlight as the service continued — outside, rather than within — the church's familiar entrance. The organ's music transcended the brick exterior, seeming to jeer "good riddance." Rose could almost see God dusting His hands in disgust. Pangs of despair cut through her.

Would she ever be able to go to Mass again? How do other hypocrites attend church and not feel tremendous guilt and shame? Of course, she was new at this game. Maybe hypocrisy got easier as time went on.

NO, no, no, no! She could not, would not, live like this! Rose didn't know what to do but, somehow, she must find peace, or die trying.

Striding toward home, she stuffed her hands into her pockets, and immediately felt Mari's key. *Well, before conquering the problem of peace, I'd better get Mari's car to Satter.*

Squaring her shoulders, she strode purposefully down the street, wishing she didn't feel so alone. If only she could share her burden with someone. Anyone.

Rose couldn't tell Satter; he'd never speak to her again. Mrs. Baldino would faint from shock. And even though God surely knew of Papa's horrible sin, she couldn't possibly talk to Father Nick. The police were out of the question — her father would be arrested at once. Even on his sickbed.

With a sense of sadness, Rose realized there was only one person who would have understood. Mari.

Sitting inside the Packard made Rose feel close to her dead friend. Like a newsreel, she let their times together play through her mind, bittersweet and nearly unbearable; malteds and memorable meals and midnight jaunts through the cemetery. Each memory encapsulated a cherished nugget of wisdom; look deeper, love better, live braver.

She thought of Father Nick's revelation — that people impact one another, whether they want to or not.

Rose stroked the mohair seats, her fingers lingering. Had anyone affected her more positively than Mari? She didn't think so. A slight breeze blew through the open windows, rustling Rose's short curls. Tears slid into her hairline, as she let her head fall backward against the seat.

A tap on her shoulder unnerved her. Disoriented, she looked around and realized she'd fallen asleep in the Packard. After rubbing her eyes, she saw Satter peering in at her. Rose felt a rush of affection.

"I'm so glad I found you!" she said, reaching for his hand. She was heartened to see him smile.

"I believe it was *I* who found *you*, Rose."

"Oh! I guess you're right." She opened the door and scooted over, allowing Satter to get behind the wheel. "I meant to find you, though." Rose reached into her pocket and extracted Mari's key. "But, I fell asleep, instead." She handed the key to Satter. "I didn't sleep at all well, last night."

"Me, neither." He held the key against the sunlight, turning it so it glinted. "Wasn't 'til this morning that I 'membered her car. Thought I'd take it to the cemetery after her," he swallowed hard, "funeral, Tuesday." Inserting the key into the ignition, he said, "Thought maybe you'd want to ride with me." He looked sideways at Rose. "Teddy wants to ride with his Uncle Satter, and I don't want to be alone with him. Wouldn't know what to say to the little fella."

"I-I'd be honored. Tuesday? Do you know what time?"

Satter's bottom lip drooped. "Three o'clock. At Crown Funeral Home."

"I'll be there." She touched his shoulder. "Satter? I can't tell you how sorry I am."

Back at home, Rose's feelings were mixed. She'd been overjoyed to see Satter and was glad to be invited to ride with him and Teddy, in spite of the reason. And, meeting Teddy would be like seeing a part of Mari. But, after saying goodbye without so much as a kiss on the cheek, Rose realized things were different between her and Satter. There was a strain between them, now. Mari's death — murder — had changed everything.

Rose felt so tired. Curling up on her bed, she wondered if anything would ever be the same again.

The sun shone brightly on Tuesday. In the little chapel at the funeral home, the short pews were only partially filled. At the front of the room, near a podium, a simple casket was displayed.

Two large bouquets of daisies flanked the ends. Rose felt tears sting her eyes and quickly averted them.

Since Mari had only been in the valley since May, Rose assumed the majority of mourners were family. Mari was one of nine siblings, she remembered. The man and woman in the front pew had to be her parents. His jaw jutted out in a stubborn way, and brutishness carved the angles of his shoulders. Rose wouldn't want to rile the man. Mari's mother sat quietly, looking down at her lap.

Rose's heart leaped when, next to the couple, she saw a pair of round eyes peeking over the pew. The little boy surveyed the room, regarding each person seriously before moving on to the next. When his eyes lit on Rose, she nodded and gave him an encouraging smile. His somber gaze moved past her without acknowledging her greeting.

Emma Splott sat regally in the back, in her wheelchair. Her features were unreadable. She'd only known Mari for a couple of months. Did she feel any sense of loss? Cecil stood next to her with his hands deep in his pockets as he leaned against the back wall. His hair looked greasy and unkempt.

It didn't take long for Rose to see Satter wasn't present. Surely, he'd be along soon, she assured herself, and then wondered if she should ask him to sit with her. She felt a little out of place.

A mousy woman, festooned with a wide, ribboned bonnet, sat at the piano in the corner. Her thin shoulders rocked from side to side, as her fingers went from one end of the ivory keys to the other. She opened her mouth and began to sing in a reedy soprano.

In peace and joy I now depart,
Since God so wills it.
Serene and confident my heart,
Stillness fills it.

Rose sighed. If ever there was a time she wished to feel serene and confident, it was now.

At that moment, Satter sidled into her pew.

"Howdy." His face was scrubbed beneath combed hair. He wore a dark suit, whose sleeves were way too short. At least six inches of white shirt extended past the cuff.

This made Rose smile. She yearned to lean against him and feel his warmth, to take comfort in his solidness. She wanted to breathe in the pleasant mix of musk and hair tonic.

She didn't dare. That closeness was reserved for lovers. At the moment, she didn't know where she stood with Satter. She looked cautiously at the young man, searching for a sign that he still loved her, but his eyes had locked onto the casket. Rose saw his jaw tighten and loosen with emotion. Now would not be the time to broach the subject.

Chapter Twelve

"*To this day, I don't remember the ride to the cemetery, Nicky. One moment, we were climbing into the Packard, the next pulling into the cemetery.*

"*What I do remember was Teddy. Sitting next to his uncle, he finally let down his guard. Like his mother, his eyes held a hint of mischievous humor. His suit was as ill-fitting as Satter's, and he didn't wear any shoes because his stubbed toe was still wrapped in gauze. Tears threatened to fall, when I remembered why he'd stubbed his toe, and with whom. More than anything, my arms ached to take the child and kiss his shiny bowl of hair. But, even though he smiled at me, he shied away when I reached out.*

Reverend Neville intoned a prayer, as the loose gathering of people bowed their heads. It seemed, other than Rose, only Mari's kin had opted to attend the graveside service. Emma and Cecil were nowhere in sight.

Mari's casket had already been lowered into the ground. The edges of the pit looked raw, and, mounded next to it, the excavated dirt waited to mend the wound.

When the service was over, Satter took Teddy's limp hand and placed some dirt in it. Together, they joined the rest of the mourners in throwing their clumps onto the top of the casket. The hollow sound jarred Rose. She stood looking down, wanting to hold onto the last moment this world would see Mari. Satter waited patiently by an elm sapling, a short distance away.

Rose was surprised when Satter didn't drop her off at home. Instead, he turned the car toward Fruitvale. Teddy sat between them and, sometime along the way, slipped his little hand into hers. She squeezed it, her heart breaking.

When the Packard turned into a dirt driveway and pulled to a stop in front of the renovated boxcar, Rose realized she'd driven past the home several times the morning of Mari's death. Why hadn't she recognized it?

There were flowers everywhere, and tall cherry trees shaded the boxcar, softening its outline. Perhaps that's why she had missed it. She hadn't expected the makeshift abode to be so — homey.

She opened the car door, and Teddy scrambled out after her, running to a small fenced area. Rose could see goats chewing lazily in the afternoon heat.

"Where's Eleanor?" she asked, stretching her legs.

"Who?"

"Eleanor Roosevelt. You said your father had dressed her up in britches and leaned her against the outdoor privy." Rose pointed to the unaccompanied outhouse.

Satter smiled for the first time that day. "Seems, our Mari was offended by Pa's sentiments, and tossed her in the river."

Rose started to chuckle, and Satter joined in. Soon, they were roaring with laughter. Leaning against each other, tears poured down their faces. When their giggles finally tapered off, the couple noticed Teddy had returned from the goats. He looked concerned.

"Don't worry, Teddy. Your Uncle Satter isn't off his nut. Not yet, anyways." Satter picked the boy up and ruffled his hair. "Just felt good to let loose. Now," he set the boy down, and pushed him toward the driveway, "go help your grandma out of the truck."

Rose turned down the invitation to stay for supper, feeling like a second left foot. She asked Satter to take her home. He obliged with the promise to his mother that he'd be back soon.

Alone with Satter, Rose couldn't bring herself to ask the question that haunted her. Did he still care about her? Feeling shy, she gazed out the window at the passing pastoral scene. The quilted fields lifted and dipped toward the Colorado River, while mammoth rolls of hay lumbered across the landscape. Rose had the sudden urge to furiously erase the view. Sunshine and beauty should not share the same day as death. Impatiently, she shifted so her back was to the window.

"You okay?" Satter reached over and covered her hand. Rose squeezed back.

"Not really. How are *you* feeling?"

He sighed. "Sad. And mad and frustrated. Can't get nothing from the authorities." Sheepishly, he glanced at her. "Seems I've become quite a nuisance, and they've banned me from coming near the police station." His voice became singsong in imitation. "We'll contact you when we have any information, sonny."

"Have they discovered any clues, yet?" Rose held her breath.

"Naw. From what I've overheard," here he flashed her a grin, "they took fingerprints, and interviewed several people. But, nothing critical to Mari's murder has surfaced. It's as if the creep disappeared off the face of the earth!" His fingers turned white as he gripped the steering wheel. "If I had two minutes with him, why I'd — "

"Perhaps it's best to let the proper authorities handle this, Satter."

"Aw, their engines are just idlin'. They aren't interested in the likes of us, Rose." He lowered his voice. "I've been doing some detectin', myself, and I think I may have something."

"What?"

"It's too dangerous to say, right now. Wouldn't want to put an innocent in harm's way. Unless — " he looked hopefully at Rose, "you'd want to help with the detectin'."

Rose froze. To help Satter would be to condemn her father. "I-I can't."

The young man suddenly became preoccupied with the road ahead. "Why can't you?"

"Because, you aren't Dick Tracy. The police can handle this much better than two amateur detectives. Hasn't it occurred to you we could get hurt? Who knows what kind of madman did this to Mari!" She crossed her arms and stuck out her chin. "We should just leave it alone."

"Are you insane? I don't know about you, but I can't sit by and do nothing! That was my sister, in case you forgot."

"And Mari was my best friend."

A static silence prevailed until the Packard screeched to a halt in front of Rose's house. She jumped out and slammed the door. Leaning in through the window, she said, "Just leave it alone, Satter!"

"Not very likely!" With that, he floored the gas pedal. Rose barely had time to withdraw her head. She clenched her hands to keep them from shaking as she watched the car disappear.

"Rose, you're assuming Sante murdered Mari, but, based on what you've described, there's a good possibility you are mistaken."

Father Nick was sitting sideways on the organ's bench. Sheets of music were spread out vertically above the keyboard. Rose had interrupted the priest's practice with a panicked plea to speak with him. Already, she felt faint with relief. It had been a good decision to finally confess the whole story to him.

"But, who else could it be? I know what I saw."

"Do you? Sometimes, our perception of things is not the clearest. Let's think about it. First," he held up a finger, "it was very dark. And," he held up a second, "you didn't actually see your father come out of Mari's door, did you?"

Rose shook her head, wanting — needing — to grasp at these fragile offerings of hope. "No, but — "

Father Nick held up a third finger. "Even though Sante has been violent with you, I can't see him as a murderer." He leaned back, "Rose, why don't you ask your father what he was doing in Shantytown that night? You may find his answer surprising."

"But, what if he *did* kill her? Wouldn't I be in danger, too?"

"Let's ask him together, then."

Rose felt her shoulders relax. For the moment, at least, the dreaded confrontation could be put off. "He's in the hospital with pneumonia, again. In Salida. I don't know when he'll come home."

"Then, we will wait. In the meantime, my dear girl," the priest swiveled to face the waiting sheets of music, "ask our Lord to give you peace. He has everything under control, in spite of how things look."

More than a week passed without hearing from Satter. Rose was destitute. She missed him terribly, and Mari, too. She even missed Papa, and had become anxious to clear the air concerning the morning Mari was killed. The more she thought of it, the more she believed she was wrong about her father's role.

But, if Papa hadn't killed her, who did? Maybe Satter really was on to something. She decided she wanted to join him in his detecting after all. That's if he was still talking to her.

On Wednesday morning, after work, Rose stopped by J.C. Penney's, in hopes of finding Satter. Mr. Class archly informed her he'd quit the night before. No reason given, just left him in the lurch, just said goodbye and walked out the door. She quickly flew from the man's peeved face.

Standing outside the store's entrance, Rose blew out air. *Now what?* With no means of finding Satter, she walked toward home.

Like that stormy night months ago, she found herself standing in the alley, looking at Mari's door in Shantytown. Someone was already moving in. Emma leaned predatorily on her crutch and talked with a young woman whose long, brown curls fell becomingly down her back. She looked a bit frightened.

Huh, I don't blame you. Watch out for that one!

She saw him as soon as she opened the door.

"Papa!" Running to him, she wrapped her arms around her father. "I've missed you." She pulled a chair close and examined his face. "Didn't they feed you in that hospital? You look half-starved!" She hopped up. "Let me fix you some food, Papa. We need to get your strength back."

Her father remained silent, but watched her with solemn eyes. Rose quickly put together a cold salad. She set it in front of her father, and then sat next to him again. He looked at her for a moment before lifting his fork.

"Mmm. This is good, er, Daughter." He cleared his throat.

Astonished, Rose reached for his forehead. "Papa? Are you feverish?"

Her father brushed her hand away, but with gentleness. "No, I am not sick, Rose. Just — changed." He put down his fork, and looked at his plate.

"What are you saying, Papa?"

"I'm beginning to see what a beast I've been to you. I've not been a good father or provider for you." His voice broke. "Can you forgive me?"

Rose sat back in shock. What was happening here? Was she dreaming? She pinched her palm. No, not dreaming.

"Why, Papa, what-?" She shook her head in wonder. "What has happened to you?"

"I nearly died there, Rose. They say I was delirious, I don't know. Rose, something happened to me in the hospital. I'm almost afraid to say it aloud." Her father peered at her, as if gauging how much he'd be believed. After a moment, he nodded.

"Maria Rosa came to me."

Rose gasped.

"It's true. She was so beautiful, so radiant! But she was not happy with me. She asked me why there was no laughter in our house, no roses blooming on the fences? And — here she was especially stern — why had I alienated our precious daughter? I was so ashamed.

"I don't know how long I was delirious, but the nurses thought the end was near, so they sent for a priest. Father Bertrand, your Father Nick, came to administer Last Rites. As he prayed, the fever left me. Sanity returned and Maria Rosa departed." He rubbed the stubble on his face. "It was difficult to say goodbye, again."

"But, to see Mama! What a miracle, Papa."

"Yes, Father Bertrand said so, too." He looked down at his hands. "He also said you think I'm a killer."

"Papa, I — "

Her father waved her explanation away. "Suffice it to say I am not the best of men, but a murderer I am not. After Father Bertrand explained what you saw, I understand why you'd think such a thing. Do you want to hear what happened that night?"

Mutely, Rose nodded.

"I was furious. Angrier than I'd ever been because what that girl said rang true. I was a bully, but I didn't want to face the truth. And," his voice slowed in sadness, "I saw, after years of trying to make this house a home, you were giving up. Finding a life outside these walls."

He surveyed the room, bleakly. Rose stretched out her hand and laid it on her father's. He picked it up and touched it to his lips.

"Where would this foolish old man be without you? I panicked. I went to see the girl. I was going to have it out with her — tell her to leave you alone. That you belonged to me. But when I got there, no one answered my banging. I looked through the window and saw the girl, bare-breasted on the bed. She looked dead. I got scared and fled, and you — you know the rest." He seemed to wilt. "Believe me, Rose. This is God's truth."

"I believe you, Papa. And I'm so glad!"

Rose polished the pews in record time, and begged to leave early. Bounding down Main Street, joy sprung from each step. She must find Satter! Now, she could help him find the real killer. The real killer. All night, she'd tried to figure out who would want Mari dead. With the fear of her father's guilt out of the way, one possibility leapt to mind.

She stopped in the Hotel D'Hamburger to ask Olive Blackburn if she'd seen Satter.

"You mean that mopey young man, over yonder?" the waitress bellowed, pointing to the farthest booth.

They saw each other at the same time. For an instant, Satter's face lit up, but then it reformed into studied aloofness.

"Hello, Rose," he said stiffly, when she approached him. He picked up a straw and examined it closely.

Rose wasn't having any of it. She pushed him over and sat next to him. "Hi!"

"I don't see anything to be happy about."

"Now, don't get your shirt in a tizzy."

"That's *wad*."

"What?"

"Don't get your shirt in a wad."

"Oh." She couldn't hold back any longer. "I think I know who killed her."

This got his attention. "Well, now you're cooking with gas! Tell me everything!"

Their heads together, Olive came up and set two chocolate malteds in front of the couple. They looked up, surprised.

"On the house," she said. "For Mari," she added, wistfully.

As it turned out, they both had the same suspect in mind. Cecil. He was jealous and, on more than one occasion, they'd heard him threaten Mari. They agreed the man needed close watching.

Against Sister Mary Bernadine's wishes, Rose took Friday off. The next two days, the couple shadowed Cecil. Satter bedded down outside the boxcar and left moments after Cecil, each morning at seven o'clock. Satter followed in the Packard a half-mile behind Cecil's old Chevy, until the man parked his car behind Shantytown. Satter parked across the street, by the LaCourt Hotel.

Rose walked a circuitous route from Little Italy and furtively joined Satter inside the Packard. Scrunched down in the front seat, they hoped they wouldn't be noticed.

First thing, Cecil disappeared through Emma's door, and after fifteen minutes, reappeared outside with a piece of paper in his hand. The couple assumed it was his list of chores for the day. Throughout the day, the man washed cars, pulled weeds, washed windows, and repaired screens. He performed his tasks carefully, but frequently panned the surrounding area, as if expecting calamity to tap him on the shoulder.

It didn't take long to convince the couple they'd found Mari's murderer. His shifty behavior shouted of guilt.

Both Friday and Saturday nights, after Emma checked his work, Cecil drove to the Copeco and didn't come out until near midnight. Fighting sleep, Satter and Rose waited until Cecil had left the lot, before starting the Packard and following. Cecil's car wove dangerously back and forth across the pavement all the way to Fruitvale.

"Drink's gonna kill that fella before the electric chair has a chance to," Satter said, disgustedly.

When Satter deposited Rose at her door in the wee hours of Sunday morning, she begged off surveillance for the day in order to attend Mass. Earlier, she had requested to leave the Copeco and be dropped at St. Joe's for confession. Satter had insisted on waiting until she'd finished. Cecil wasn't going anywhere, he'd said.

A day off was fine with Satter, for he'd learned from his mother that Cecil didn't work on Sunday, and stayed home. If he happened to leave, Satter assured Rose, he would follow the villain alone.

At Mass, Rose went forward with the rest of the congregation. It felt good. Shaking hands with Father Nick after the service, she thanked him profusely for helping heal her relationship with her father.

He bestowed a benign smile on her. "Nothing is impossible with the Lord, Rose."

She now believed that with her whole heart.

A horn sounded outside, while Rose prepared a supper tray. It was Sunday evening. Papa was again feeling poorly, and had taken to bed. She poked her head out the front door and was surprised to see Satter. She waved at him, indicating she'd be with him in a few minutes. Before picking up the tray of chicken soup and warm rolls, she tweaked the napkin's edge so it lay flat. With a soft knock, she opened her father's door and put a smile on her face.

"I made you some soup, Papa. Your favorite."

Her father's face was ashen, and dark circles had reappeared under his rheumy eyes. Rose hid her concern behind cheery chatter. Placing the tray next to her father, she encouraged him to sit up and take a spoonful. He obliged with great effort, giving her a weary smile.

"You're too good to me, Rose."

"Fiddlesticks. Now, eat Papa." She held the spoon to his lips, and he sipped the broth. After several sips, color began to seep back into his face.

"Good," Rose said, pulling the blanket up to her father's chin. She placed the half-empty bowl back on the tray. *A little is better than nothing.* She leaned over and kissed his brow. He closed his eyes and sighed.

"I love you, Rose."

"I love you, too, Papa." Picking up the tray, she quietly exited the room, whispering a prayer for his speedy recovery.

"What's the occasion?"

"Our bird has left his nest." Satter winked. "Needed my side-kick. Hey, what's the matter, doll?"

"Dr. Monro said it would take a while for Papa to get his strength back, but I'm a little worried. He seems to be getting worse, not better. My gallivanting all over town probably isn't helping. I should be nursing him back to health, like a good Italian girl."

"I'm sorry, Rose. Maybe you should stay here, tonight. It's getting dangerous, anyway." Satter looked both ways and lowered his voice. "I think Cecil saw me following him. If he suspects something, well — I'd kick myself if you got hurt."

"No, Satter, I'm sure Papa will be all right. We're in this together."

Satter leaned over and kissed her cheek. "When did you leave heaven, Rose?"

Rose blushed, as he started the Packard and drove down the street. Her gaze lingered on her house for a moment before she turned her attention to the evening's itinerary.

"Hey, why are we going to Shantytown?"

"Our man's there."

"Isn't it his day off? What business would he have there today?"

"That's what we're gonna find out."

He parked in their usual place, but instead of waiting inside the Packard, Satter quietly opened the door and slipped out. Rose followed on his heels. Her pulse had quickened, uncomfortably.

"What are we doing, Satter?"

"Shh. We're gonna spy on them."

"On whom?"

"Leave it to a woman to ask so many questions!" Satter softened his criticism with a light chuckle. "Come on, silly. Trust me."

"But, it's not even dark. We'll be seen!"

"Not if we're careful." He took her hand and they stayed close to the side of Emma's house. He pulled her down below Emma's open kitchen window, a feathery pink tamarisk bush hiding them from questioning eyes. Emma's radio was playing loudly.

"What's the idea of breaking in here in the middle of my singing?"

"Singing? When you set that croup to music and call it singing, you've gone too far!"

"Now look here, Allen, I don't care what you say about my singing on your own program, but after all, I've got listeners!"

"Keep your family out of this."

Satter mouthed, "Jack Benny." Tinny laughter poured from the radio. Rose nodded. She was familiar with the Jell-O Program and Mr. Benny's mock anti-Fred Allen jokes. She always joined the Baldino family on Sunday night to listen and chuckle with the rest of America. This was the first time she'd heard the two famous men swap insults on the same show, though.

"Another crack like that and Town Hall will be looking for a new janitor."

Rose muffled a giggle, when Satter squeezed her arm. Agitated voices had moved close to the window above them. Too close. Rose recognized Emma and Cecil, and tried to make herself smaller. It would surely mean death if they were discovered hovering below the sill. She looked anxiously at her companion for direction. He was listening intently.

"I'm only giving you half, Cecil."

The man's voice rose to a shrill pitch. "Listen here, ya double crossin', rusty ol' hen! Ya ain't leavin' me holdin' the bag. I gotta git outta here, an' fast. Now, gimme the lettuce, er they'll be tossin' ya in the meatwagon, too!" Rose could almost see Cecil looming over the old woman, trying to frighten her. Rose was certainly quivering with fear.

"Ya botched the job, an' I had to finish it. Ya'll not git one more penny outta me, mister!" Emma's voice not only didn't sound frightened, it was mule stubborn. And, Rose realized, it had lost its strange accent. Strains of pure Missouri Mountain Folk spilled unhindered through the window. "Ya kin peddle yer papers elsewhere, buddy."

So much for Her Majesty's highfaluting ways! Rose started to share her disdain, and discovered she was alone under the sill. She heard a loud noise, as Emma's front door crashed open. Rose peeked over the sill and saw Satter standing in the doorway, heaving in rage.

"Why? Mari never hurt you, you old bat!"

"Well now, ain't the names aflyin' tonight? Cecil, how 'bout ya take care o' this annoyin' fly?"

Rose gasped when she saw Cecil rush toward Satter. Satter neatly sidestepped the man and smashed his fist into his temple. Cecil crumpled. The wad of paper money he'd held blossomed like a green flower on the rug.

A long sigh escaped from Emma. "Seems a job ain't done lest ya do it yerself. Watch it, mister!"

Satter stopped in mid-stride when he saw the gun. The old woman had extracted it from the folds of her robe and was pointing it at his chest. He lifted his hands slowly.

Rose was furious. How dare this tart of a woman threaten her Satter? She rose, poised to jump through the window and rescue him. Satter saw her and gave her a miniscule shake of his head. She froze.

Well, what do you want me to do?

As if reading her mind, he flicked his eyes to the left, indicating she should leave. Get the police.

"No need to tack another murder to your behind, Emma. Let's talk about it." He inched toward the old woman.

Rose had reached the corner of the bungalow, hurrying to fulfill Satter's telepathic order, when she heard a gunshot.

"Satter!" Within seconds, she was at Emma's door, pulling it open. She leaped over the prostrate Cecil and ran toward the two bodies, wrestling on the floor.

"No you don't!"

She pulled Emma off Satter, untangling her fingers from their death grip on his hair. The old woman's face was distorted beyond recognition. She snarled like an enraged animal. Rose didn't know how she did it, but she held Emma's ferocity at bay, while she rolled Satter over. He was hurt. Groaning, he sat up and reached for his arm, where a red stain was spreading.

Where he'd been pinned to the floor, a gun lay. Emma and Rose both reached for it, but Rose got there first. Immediately, she pointed the gun at Emma, her hand surprisingly steady, her finger desperate to pull the trigger.

This was the closest she'd come to truly hating anyone, and a strange energy exploded in her. She grappled with the crushing desire to take this woman's life, like Emma had done to Mari. But, Rose knew, there would be no living with herself if she did. Reluctantly, she lowered the gun.

As she did, Emma's mouth twisted into a triumphant smirk. For a moment, Rose just stared. The next moment, Emma was unconscious on the floor. Rose rubbed her fist.

"For a good Italian girl, you sure pack a punch. Mari couldn't have done it better."

Satter grinned proudly, while Rose helped him stand up. She could see he was trying not to grimace with pain as he leaned against her. With gentle hands, she rearranged his wounded arm. When she heard a sharp intake of breath, she looked up, worried she'd hurt him.

"Cecil's gone."

Rose spun her head around and saw the screen door shutting. "He won't get far."

Chapter Thirteen

"So, they cracked under pressure and spilled the beans. Sheriff Lumley predicts they'll get life at hard labor. At least, that's what he told Ma and Pa."

"Humph. As old as Emma is, that won't be nearly long enough to pay for what she did! And, Cecil, well . . ."

"Even death's too good for the likes of them!"

The couple was sitting in a booth at the Hotel D'Hamburger, eating dinner. Satter's right arm hung in a sling. Eating his hamburger one-handed was clumsy, and frequently, he'd put it down to lick juice off his fingers. Rose stuffed a French-fried potato into his open mouth, before picking one out for herself. She dipped it in a glob of catsup and smacked her lips in anticipation.

"Tell me everything," she said, dabbing her mouth with the tip of a napkin.

"Sis was right in thinking Emma was a white-slaver. She admitted our Mari was next on her list. The authorities rounded up the main ring out of Utah, and arrested the lot. Head fella confessed Emma had kidnapped and sold them at least twenty young gals over the last few years. Maybe more."

"Why would she do such a thing?"

"The green stuff. She was afraid of being poor. When she'd left her home, as a young woman, she'd been the third generation of dirt-poor mountain folk. She'd had enough of hog gristle and cousins getting hitched. Went to California, married a fella there and eventually settled down in Oregon for a time. Even had a couple of kids.

"But, a tiger don't change its stripes. Emma deserted her family and wound up in Colorado, determined to make a new life and acquire the wealth she'd always dreamed of.

"Her plans were shaping up fine, until Mari became a threat. She'd told the old woman she'd seen some papers in her desk, and she wasn't gonna stand for her shenanigans."

Rose remembered the funny look on Mari's face when Emma had cut her hair. It was short time after, that Mari told Rose to stay away from Shantytown. Things were starting to make sense.

"The day before she was killed, Olive told me Mari had put in an application for work here. She was washing her hands of Shantytown. Not soon enough, though. Emma had already hired Cecil to kill Mari. What she hadn't counted on was Cecil being in love with his intended victim.

"The thought of taking Mari's life sickened him, but he needed the money. Was in debt up to his Adam's apple. So, he'd plied her with whiskey, and himself, too. Hoped it would give him courage. Instead of finding the courage to kill her, he became amorous.

"They were both soused, and, I'm ashamed to say, Mari agreed to take off her clothes. But then, he tried to talk her into going away with him. Not surprising, she laughed at his suggestion, which enraged him. Before he knew it, his hands had wrapped around her neck." Satter struggled to collect himself. "She blacked out within seconds, and then he realized what he'd done.

"He panicked. Snatching up the first thing he saw, her bloomers, he ran outside and sopped them under the water spigot. He doused her face and neck, but still didn't get a response. And this is the despicable part. Since he figured the worst had happened, he decided he needed a souvenir from Mari. Rummaging around in her dresser drawers, he found her scissors and snitched a coupla curls. On his way out, he grabbed a dress.

"It was just after midnight. He drove home and took refuge under the very roof of his victim's parents. May the swine rot in hell!" Satter's lip curled.

"But he *hadn't* killed her. When I found Mari — it must have been close to five, she was still alive, if just barely."

"This is where it gets crazy. Something woke Emma up." Satter shook his head in anger and disbelief. "I don't understand how someone could sleep when they know a person's life is about to be snuffed out! The woman's heart must be made of stone."

"Or ice," Rose added.

"Surely. Anyways, something woke her up. Since she was awake, she decided to check out the damage Cecil had done. But, when she'd snuck into Mari's room, she discovered our girl gasping for air. Cursing at Cecil, she took Mari's apron off the chair and wrapped the strings around her neck. Pulling with all her strength, she finished the dastardly deed, and then hobbled back to her bed."

"Oh, Satter." Rose leaned her head against his shoulder and closed her eyes. "Mari must have suffered terribly."

Satter became quiet, and Rose sensed an unusual stillness in his posture. Curious, she looked up.

"Are you all right?"

The young man chewed on his bottom lip, and then looked down at her. "Um, Rose, I do have one more thing to tell you. But, I'm afraid you'll think I've gone off my nut."

Rose sat up straight and turned so she was facing Satter. "I'd never think that!"

"Better save your opinion until after you've heard what I got to say. Ready?"

It appeared Satter was directing the question more to himself than Rose, but she nodded, anyway.

"Well, I had a dream last night. Normally, I don't ever remember my dreams, but this one has haunted me all day. I think someone is trying to tell me something." He took a deep breath.

"Go on, Satter. I'm listening."

Rose stopped talking, lost in the past.

"Don't stop now, Nonna! What was his dream about?"

Shaking herself, Rose smiled, apologetically. "Well, Nicky, Satter's dream changed my whole way of seeing death. And life.

"In this dream, Satter stood in Mari's room. He knew immediately he was revisiting the scene of the crime, sometime after Cecil had left, but before Emma's entrance. Mari lay motionless on the bed, but he sensed she was still alive. He wanted to help her, at least cover her nakedness, but found he couldn't move.

"With his voice hushed, Satter then told me that a 'beautiful creature' of some sort appeared next to him. His face shone like a thousand

suns, and a bright light washed over the tiny room. He didn't seem to notice Satter, but reached out and touched Mari. Satter watched her eyes open and was filled with joy. The creature looked at Mari with such tender love, and spoke.

"'Child, your time here is nearly over," he said. "I need to know — do you love me?'

"His voice reminded Satter of many waterfalls, Nicky, and yet it was so calm and peaceful. He looked at his sister, suddenly wanting to know what her answer was.

"She blinked, and the creature smiled, radiantly. The sound of waterfalls filled the room once more.

"'Then, welcome the arms of your Lord.'

"In a flash, the creature vanished. The room became dark, and when he could see again, Satter looked at the bed. Mari was gone, and lying across her pillow was one red rose."

A panorama of revelations rolled across Nick's face, as he finally understood what his grandmother had been trying to tell him this whole, incredible night.

"Katharine was never alone, was she, Nonna?" He began to weep.

"Not for a moment, Nicky. And neither are you." Rose reached out her arms and gathered her grandson to her.

Nine months had passed, when Satter parked the Packard in front of Rose's house for the final time. So much had happened since Mari's murder. Cecil and Emma were sent to prison to serve out their terms. That spring, Papa had died from a third bout of pneumonia, and gone to be with his beloved Maria Rosa. But, not before planting a few rose bushes. Rose had graduated from Grand Junction High School, and was making plans for the future. Since her romance with Satter had dwindled after Christmas, she'd added becoming a nun to her list of possible vocations.

She'd been washing lettuce when she heard the familiar honk. Feeling a momentary lurch in her stomach, she smoothed her apron and ran out the front door.

"Satter! What are you doing here?"

The young man caught her and swung her around before placing her gently on her feet. He put his hands on her shoulders and turned her first one way, then the other.

"You're more beautiful than I remember, Rose!"

"Oh, you flatterer!" She laughed, pulling on her earlobe. "Can you stay for a while? We could sit on the porch and talk." She winked. "Mrs. Baldino has taken her kids, and rolling pin, to visit her sister in Fruita."

Satter looked like he might accept her invitation, but then shook his head. "Naw, Rose. Actually, I'm on my way out of town."

"Oh." It was then Rose noticed the suitcase sitting on the Packard's running board. "Did you drive all the way over here with your suitcase like that?"

"Actually, I — "

Rose started walking toward the Packard. Satter followed. Opening the passenger door, she slid in. "Lots of memories in this car, huh? I'll be sad to see it go."

"Well, Rose, that's what I wanted to talk to you about. See," he cleared his throat, "I'm just a wandering man. Having a vehicle to take care of, well, that would only tie me down." Satter sat on his heels next to the open door. He rested his hand on the suitcase. "I have a feeling Mari would like this idea I got. And I hope you do, too."

"He just gave you Mari's car?"

Rose nodded. "He said Mari would have enjoyed the idea of help-ing me get out of town and start a new life somewhere. As long as I had her car, he told me, I could go whereever my heart desired and Mari's memory could go along for the ride."

Nick had already returned the folding chair to the back seat of the Packard, and tossed the dirty coveralls, shovel, and canvas bag into the trunk. The sun had risen above George Crawford's mausoleum, send-ing long shards of light through the trees. Nonna leaned on her walker, shoulders slumped in exhaustion. Nick came up beside her.

"And it's been quite a ride, Nonna."

"It's not over yet, boy!"

"You mean—?"

Rose looked up at her grandson with a twinkle in her eye. "She's all yours, now."

Nick kissed his grandmother's brow, and then joined her in admiring his handiwork. For over a half century, Mari's gravesite had been neglected and poorly marked. Reflecting the new dawn, a shiny marble headstone rested comfortably in the earth, a long overdue obligation — finally satisfied. It said:

Here lies Marietta Monroe
Born March, 1915
Died August, 1937
Beloved Daughter, Sister, Mother
And Friend

The Real Story

I first learned about Jeanette Morris on the Orchard Mesa Cemetery Tour led by Grand Junction's illustrious historian and Colorful Character, Dave Fishell. Her story was one of many fascinating stops during the tour.

As we ambled over to an obscure grave, our group was told of the notorious 1937 Apron String Murder, where a prostitute was found strangled one morning on the seedy side of town. Her death had caused a small furor at the time, and then was quickly forgotten, until resurrected by Mr. Fishell.

Although, Jeanette Morris stood out as one of the more interesting dead, it wasn't until a second tour several years later that she became an obsession to me. The reason? In the interim, a marble headstone had replaced her little marker.

Who would do such a thing sixty years after the death of a lowly prostitute? When asked, Mr. Fishell said no one knew. The headstone had just appeared overnight. The mind of this writer was now acutely intrigued, and I knew I would have to write Jeanette's story.

I never thought I'd find out who mysteriously replaced that marker, but this writer's imagination ran amuck with delicious possibilities. But, where to start? I reined in my enthusiasm and decided to get to know the victim. Perhaps, I would find my story when I had a few more details.

My first stop was the Museum of Western Colorado to visit my friends, Judy Prosser-Armstrong and Sissi Williams. In the archives I found my first information about the murder. It was my first look at Jeanette, too.

A blurry photograph of her naked and lifeless body was printed next to arrest shots of Cecil McHolland and W.D.

Miller. Though the barest of details were given, at least now, I had names, dates, and pictures. My appetite was whetted. After thanking my friends, I was off to the library.

Mesa County Public Library is staffed with accommodating people, and they pointed out a plethora of media in which to find facts about Grand Junction's history. I found the most helpful for my needs was the *Daily Sentinel Newspaper* on microfilm.

I spent the afternoon perusing the month of August 1937, and finally came to the day I was interested in. August 14.

22-Year-Old Girl Strangled To Death In City's Notorious Barbary Coast District; CCC Enrollee Is Held As Suspect

The *Daily Sentinel* article began, *"Jeanette Morris, 22 years of age, and the daughter of Clarence C. Jones, residing a mile and a quarter east of the State Home, was found dead at 6:30 this morn-ing in her room at the Jennie Ward home, 133 Colorado Avenue, where she had been employed as a housekeeper and chauffeur for the past three or four weeks."*

What? Not a prostitute? I pored over that and ensuing articles, which described the scene of the crime, the details (as they were known then) of Jeanette's movements the night before (eerily, Friday, the 13th), what was known of her life, including her char-acter, interviews with family, and who Henry Anderson (the sus-pect) was and why he was suspected.

It was reported that Jeanette's body was lying across her bed in her shanty, and was naked from the waist up with a soaking wet garment, later identified as bloomers, lying across her neck. The reporter surmised this showed someone had tried to revive her after finding out she was dead or unconscious. She had bruises on her neck and an apron string was tied around her neck, tight enough to leave an indention. There were finger bruises and teeth marks on her body, too.

The bedroom was first reported not in disorder, indicating there had not been a struggle. Her clothing was found on the floor, evidently where it had been dropped when she disrobed.

Two locks of hair had been removed from Jeanette's head. One was found under her body, the other was missing. The scissors lay near her on the bed.

There were disturbing discrepancies. Jennie Ward, who found Jeanette around 6:30 in the morning, said the room appeared in order, yet drawers were pulled out and flung on the floor, the screen was torn, and even though there were clothes on the floor, the dress Jeanette had worn the night before seemed to be missing. The apron string was both reported as tied tightly around her neck and crossed loosely. Jennie Ward said she didn't notice the wet garment across Jeanette's neck, yet, when she found her, she had shaken the woman. Awfully close not to notice a wet garment across her neck. Some reports said Jeanette was half-naked, others said she was completely unclothed. Jennie Ward said she'd pulled a sheet up to cover Jeanette before calling the police, which may be why the details of her nudity was confused.

On August 16th, the coroner's jury found Jeanette Morris had met her death by strangulation, feloniously, at the hands of some unknown person or persons at some unknown place between the hours of 8 p.m. Friday, August 13th and 6 a.m. Saturday, August 14th.

Medical examination practically eliminated the possibility the slaying may have been the work of a "sexual pervert," and no evidence was brought out to show jealousy may have prompted the killing.

Authorities also said they were not convinced Jeanette was killed in her room. They believed the actual murder took place around midnight. When she was examined around 7 a.m. the morning of the murder, the doctors found she'd been dead around seven hours.

Jeanette's murder remained unsolved for nearly a year and a half, although several men were brought in for questioning, including the man who, when brought in over a year later, confessed to her murder.

In March of 1939, two men were arrested for the murder of Jeanette Morris. Cecil McHolland, a twenty-five year old married man and father, and W.D. Miller, a fifty-two year old husband and former Fuller Brush salesman, were brought in by a Special Investigator from Denver, Walter Byron.

There were several attempts at getting the facts right, with the two men giving false confessions. The final confession was used in McHolland's trial, March 29, 1939, presided over by District Judge George W. Bruce, out of Montrose. Miller's trial was set for a later time.

Judge Bruce's courtroom was cleared due to the, "nature of the testimony about to be heard in the case." Only court attaches, members of the victim's immediate family, and newspapermen were allowed to stay.

On the stand, McHolland admitted he and Miller picked Jeanette up early in the evening of August 13, and drove around with her. They said they took the girl home around midnight, and remained with her for some time while attempting amorous relations with her. All three had consumed a large quantity of wine and later some whiskey during the evening. All three were sitting on the bed most of the time.

Finally, McHolland got to his feet, paced the floor a few times, and then criticized Jeanette for not paying more attention to him. By this time, he confessed, Jeanette was partially undressed. Miller expressed a desire to leave the place and got up from the bed. Jeanette and McHolland were standing up and, a moment later, were tussling with McHolland's hands about her throat. They fell over onto the bed, the youth's hands still around her throat. He reproached Jeanette for, "running around to dances with other fellows."

Soon Jeanette became insensible. Miller said he witnessed the scene and asked McHolland, "What the hell are you trying to do?"

McHolland replied, "I guess I've already done it."

McHolland testified he choked Jeanette with his hands and that, "I didn't know what I was doing because I was pretty drunk." He told the jury he became incensed at Jeanette and warned her, "If you're going to be my girl, I don't want you running around with other fellows." He denied he used an apron string in choking her. Yet, in one of his false confessions, he said he'd strangled her with a "string."

As the girl lay "lifeless" on the bed, McHolland went for a "rag" to use as a "sponge" in an effort to revive her. Miller said McHolland obtained some water outside the room, and attempted to revive Jeanette. Meanwhile, he had clipped a lock of hair from the girl's tousled head, and placed it on the washstand, later putting it in his pocket.

The two men didn't know how Jeanette became completely unclothed, but agreed that she was undressed when they left the room. Her dress was lying on the floor when her body was found. Another dress, one first believed she had worn that evening, was missing from the room.

Jenny Ward testified at the trial that she'd found Jeanette's nude body stretched across a bed in one of the rooms of Mrs. Ward's property at 133 Colorado Avenue. She described the victim's head hanging over the edge of the bed. Clothes were scattered over the room, and drawers of a commode or dresser were pulled out and lay on the floor. She did not see a wet rag lying on the girl's face nor an apron string around her neck "at the time." Neither did she notice that locks of hair had been clipped from her head. She did not know if Jeanette was in her room when the former retired the night before, and she didn't remember whether or not anyone came to see Jeanette in the evening.

Other witnesses included Investigator Byron, Under Sheriff E.A. Ingram, Detective Joe Keith, Sheriff Charles Lumley, Former Police Chief Decker, and the doctors who performed the post mortem, Drs. Jaros and Munro.

One key witness was Jeanette's younger brother, Richard Jones, who was reportedly the last to see the victim alive. The night before Jeanette was discovered murdered, they had been waiting on Main Street, outside the Hotel D'Hamburger, for Jeanette's boyfriend, J.D. Lumpkin, to get off work. They had plans to go to a movie together. Richard testified that when a car pulled up near them, someone called from the car to Jeanette, and she went over to it. When she came back, she told Richard to tell Lumpkin she was ill and going home. Then she got in the car, and it drove off. He was unable to identify the occupants. It was the last time he saw his sister.

During the trial, some interesting questions were raised concerning certain evidence. Special Investigator Byron said that nothing said so far had cleared up the point regarding an apron found on the bed, of which the strings had been wrapped around the victim's throat. According to the statements, nothing of the sort was used by McHolland, who said he choked the girl with his hands.

Also, Dr. E.E.H. Munro could not say definitely whether death was due to pressure on the throat by a person's hands or to the tightly drawn apron string.

Of interest, when answering the question, "Would it take more or less strength to strangle a person if that person were intoxicated?" Dr. Munro replied that it would be, "easier if he were intoxicated." Since Cecil was a small person and Jeanette weighed about 175 pounds and was muscular, this may explain how Jeanette could have been overpowered.

A flowered crepe dress was produced while Mrs. Jennie Ward was on the stand, and the witness identified it, "as the one worn by Jeanette on August 13," and also as the one that lay on the floor near the bed when the murder was discovered by Mrs. Ward. The dress became People's Exhibit A. Other exhibits entered by the state were a "woman's undergarment," identified as the wet cloth lying on Jeanette's body, the apron string which witnesses said had been drawn around her throat, a pair of scissors found near the bed, a lock of hair from Jeanette's head — found on the bed by the officers, a picture of the body taken by former Chief of Police, H.E. Decker, and a small photograph of Jeanette taken a short time before her death for her chauffeur's license.

The District Attorney, W.F. Haywood, asked the jury if they had, "any conscientious scruples against infliction of the death penalty." Should McHolland be convicted of first-degree murder, as charged, the jury was required to fix the punishment at life imprisonment or death. No one had a problem with that.

Defense Attorney, William Raso, concluded in his arguments, that McHolland was a "victim of circumstances." He continued by stating rape had not been intended, there were conflicting stories, and that McHolland wasn't a hardened criminal. "It appears this mystery has not entirely been solved." Raso asked the jury not to give McHolland the death penalty.

Haywood called these arguments absurd. "This is a case, if we ever had one, where the death penalty should be invoked."

The jury didn't agree, and McHolland was sentenced to life in prison. But, what the jury did next surprised everyone.

After weighing the evidence, the jury agreed on the verdict around 7 a.m. They presented the judge with an unusual statement after announcing their verdict. It read:

"Upon pronouncement of sentence of life imprisonment in the state penitentiary at hard labor, we wish to express our dissatisfaction with what, under our present laws, this sentence implies. We realize that under our present laws, this defendant will, at some future date, if his conduct warrants, become eligible for parole. We feel life imprisonment should mean just that — life imprisonment.

"Realizing that it is not in the province of this jury to dictate the enforcement of the present statutes of Colorado, we do wish to go on record as recommending the most careful scrutiny to any application by the defendant at some probably future date for parole."

Miller's trial began the 13th of April. The jury was bound by the constraints of either finding Miller guilty of murder in the first degree, or guilty of manslaughter. If he were found not guilty of either of these, he would be a free man.

Council for the defendant, John Banks, brought up several questions to be considered. He denied, "that this case has been completely solved," and argued that, "the State had not disproved a theory someone returned to Mrs. Morris' room after the murder was alleged to have been committed.

"Why was the screen door to the room torn? And why haven't they shown why this girl's dress wasn't torn, in spite of the struggle alleged to have occurred?"

Although the doctor stated the girl had been dead several hours when he examined the body about 6:45 a.m., it was brought out in Miller's trial that her body was still warm when she was found, which could lead one to speculate she may have been killed later than when McHolland and Miller had left her.

Banks made a point to ask the jury, "Why haven't they shown why her body was still warm at 6:45 a.m. when the evidence shows Miller and McHolland left the room about 12:30 a.m.?"

Most importantly, it was stated no testimony in either trials had thus cleared up the matter of the apron strings.

Miller did not testify on his own behalf, but in his confession acknowledged being in the room at the time of McHolland's attack on Jeanette, and corroborated McHolland's testimony. It was interesting that neither man seemed to know Jeanette was dead when they left the shanty.

Two days later, Miller was acquitted, much to the dismay of the citizens of Grand Junction. There was an angry editorial about it in the *Daily Sentinel,* which eventually led to a Grand Jury focused on routing crime out of the city.

Banks' questions struck me as reasonable, and I began thinking there was more to this story than met the eye. After reading and rereading the dozens of articles, I started putting ideas down on paper for my book. Initially, I thought it should be non-fiction, so everyone would know the truth about Jeanette.

Going on that premise, I went to the Mesa County Courthouse and tried to find information on the McHolland trial. The clerk did some checking and gave me the box number of the court documents filed at the State Archives in Denver. With today's forensics, I was hoping to find the doctor's reports and crime scene analyses and show them to the coroner. I was hoping this information could prove or disprove what Banks inferred — that there was someone who came along after McHolland and Miller left, and finished the botched job.

Within weeks, I drove to Denver and settled myself at a table with a medium sized box in front of me. This was better than Christmas morning! The first thing I pulled out was the transcript, and met my greatest disappointment. Every page was written in shorthand! And, nary a translation in sight. It was only later, I found out transcripts weren't transcribed unless an appeal had been filed. Daunted, but not hopeless, I reached in the box again.

What I pulled out left me stunned. Although, most of the People's Exhibits had been either given back or disposed of, three important items remained.

It was when I touched Jeanette's lock of hair (P.E. "E") that she became a living, breathing person to me. I couldn't take my eyes off her hair. Bleached of some of its original darkness and laced with split ends, it was held together by a bobby pin. The only thing left on earth, outside of a casket, that was quintessentially Jeanette.

It was hard to let loose of the lock of hair, but I finally put it down and picked up the next item. I held the original photo of Jeanette's naked and lifeless body, taken by former Police Chief Decker the morning she was discovered murdered. It was the same one I saw at the museum and the same one printed on the front page of the *Daily Sentinel*, March 29, 1939. The blurriness was gone, and now the fine details of a life snuffed out before its time was clear.

I could see Jeanette's breasts that once nurtured a son. Her clothes lay haphazardly on the floor, a pair of white dress shoes prominent in the forefront, as if thoroughly expecting to be donned that day, as usual. The dreadful apron was bunched loosely beneath her head, the strings wrapped around her neck. Tears sprung to my eyes.

When I picked up the third item, another picture, my astonishment was complete. It was Jeanette's chauffeur's license picture. Ruefully, I acknowledged, even back in the thirties, unbecoming driver's license pictures had been the norm. But, seeing Jeanette's eyes alive and open, her smile reminiscent of Mona Lisa, a connection to this long dead woman was forged.

When I returned to Grand Junction, with photocopies of the pictures, Jeanette's hair, and thirty pages of the transcript, I went about trying to find someone who could decipher the shorthand. I put an ad in the paper, which netted many interested women, all of which looked at the sample I brought by and scratched their heads. Then I discovered there were two different styles of shorthand used in courts, Gregg and Pitman. Which was *my* transcript?

Back to the library, where I picked up a book on Gregg Shorthand, I had to order one on Pitman Shorthand from another library. I first started with the Gregg and, after rubbing my temples, decided I was too old to start learning a foreign language. None of the penciled scratches matched the Gregg book. When I got the Pitman handbook, I tried again. Ureka!

One of the hieroglyphics in the transcript I guessed was the address, 133 Colorado. I compared the symbol with "Colorado" in the handbook, and it was a match. At least now I knew what I was dealing with.

My enthusiasm deflated quickly when I found out there was only one person in the United States who knew Pitman, and she was unavailable. Apparently, Pitman was archaic in our country. Amazingly, one of the ladies who had responded to my ad offered to *learn* Pitman to help me. It seemed Jeanette had garnered another fan. Unfortunately, Nancy Thrailkill, though making incredible progress, was unable to decipher the script, either. To her, it looked like it had been written left-handed, making the nuances difficult to read. It was back to the drawing board.

Eventually my searching led me to Elizabeth Titherington, a court reporter who used Pitman regularly. She was a native of Liverpool, England who lived in Canada, but was on a work program in the United States. She offered to "give it a go." But, after months of trying, she gave up, too. Though no progress with the transcript, Elizabeth and I remain good friends to this day.

So, where to go next? I decided writing a non-fiction account of Jeanette's murder was too sketchy, and began an outline for a fictionalized version.

One day, while reading the paper, I saw that the Grand Junction High School Class of 1939 was meeting for their sixtieth reunion. Since this was close to the year Jeanette died, it occurred to me I could fictionalize Jeanette's story within a larger story about Grand Junction in the 1930s.

Alice Else became my new best friend. She introduced me to several people who allowed themselves to be interviewed about life during the Depression. Many of their poignant remembrances are recounted in *Stained Glass Rose*. Since my interviews, several of these dear people have passed away. I am thankful for having met them.

One day, at the computer, I had this strange urge to find out how heavy a headstone really was. I called the first number I saw,

Snyder Memorials. I told the woman why I was calling, and told her about the mysterious headstone that had appeared overnight. There was a momentary silence on the line, and then she said something that stopped my heart. She believed she knew who might have purchased that headstone.

Her information led me to several of Jeanette's relatives. Before I knew it, I was interviewing people in Georgia, Washington, Oregon, and Colorado. My most exciting conversation was with Richard Jones, the brother who had last seen his sister alive. He was happy to share every detail that he could remember about that last night and Jeanette's murder. He also shared what happened to the family after the murder. Much of this information, as well as what I gleaned from Jeanette's sisters, has been woven through the scenes and characters in *Stained Glass Rose,* and the story is richer for it. Much of Jeanette is reflected in the character of Mari.

Richard remembered several things that never came out in the papers, or was never known to the public. Shortly before her death, Jeanette had shared some fears concerning her employer. These remarks and the fact that Jeanette had placed an application for waitress work at the Hotel D'Hamburger the week before, made Richard suspicious after his sister's death. He has his own thoughts about the mystery of the apron strings, and who might have used them.

Another thing that rankled him was his sister being labeled a prostitute, when she had simply taken a housekeeping/chauffeur job with Mrs. Ward. I did find an ad in the *Daily Sentinel,* the beginning of July, for such a job at 133 Colorado, Mrs. Ward's establishment. This validated Richard's remark, in my opinion.

He remembers Jeanette as a jolly, heavy-set girl with a beautiful smile and eyes that twinkled. She was a hard worker, experienced in farm work and preferred to clean out stables and work with horses. The account of Mari breaking in a mule wasn't far off from the real story. Richard, May, and Thelma all agreed Jeanette could be like a bull in a china closet, and May laughed over Jeanette's tendency to use every pan in the house when she cooked.

Jeanette had a son by her first marriage. Fred was four when his mother was killed, and lived with his grandparents until his

Aunt May and her husband, Hank, became his guardians. Fred went into the service at the age of seventeen, and remains close to his aunt and uncle.

I was impressed by Jeanette's relatives and how they had handled her death. Her parents moved away, but returned in the forties and ran a greenhouse just across the street from the cemetery their daughter was buried in. Fred remembers playing near his mother's grave. Richard, who'd basically been on his own since he was seven, enlisted in the Army at the age of fifteen. He served his country in Special Services. Marrying right after the war, he and a partner began a construction company that eventually made him a millionaire several times over. His beloved wife of nearly fifty years died, and he eventually remarried a "wonderful lady."

Thelma, another sister, lives on the Grand Mesa. She sent me an attractive picture of Jeanette, sitting next to J.D. Lumpkin and another girl, on a boulder on the Grand Mesa. This was taken six weeks before she was murdered. It is unsettling to notice a band of shadow across her neck, as if a premonition of what was to come.

For three years, I worked on bringing *Stained Glass Rose* to print. My journey brought me in contact with many wonderful people, most importantly, Jeanette Morris. I have come to love her, and it is my hope that my book honors her memory, as well as the character and personality God gave her, so much of which never was understood or appreciated.

Mrs. Jennie Ward died in the mid-nineteen forties. Her obituary included an interesting tidbit. It said she attended the "Church of the Golden Rule." There was no such listing under churches in the city listings. The Grand Jury, and time, finally had their way. Not too many years later, the "notorious Barbary Coast District" no longer existed. Today, its murky ghosts lay beneath a new parking lot next to Two Rivers Convention Center.

I've been unable to find what became of Cecil McHolland, but in April of 1949, the same judge who presided over McHolland's trial, Judge Bruce, wrote a letter to Mrs. Lucy Hogan, Clerk of District Court. He asked her to remind him of the details of McHolland's case. He stated Cecil's record was good in the penitentiary, and if he could give him any assistance in getting a parole, he'd be glad to make a recommendation. I haven't been able to find out if McHolland was released then or later.

There were rumors that W.D. Miller became a barber and moved to a small mountain town in the Rockies.

Oh, and the new headstone? In 1997, after retiring on the West Coast, Fred Rule decided to visit his mother's grave on his way to Georgia, where his son and daughter-in-law lived. It was extremely difficult to find the grave, and he decided it was time for his mother to have a decent headstone. Although Richard had sent money for a headstone to his parents many years before, the money got spent on something else. So, Fred purchased the headstone before heading out to Georgia, his new home — sixty years after his mother's death.

Little did he know what that simple, loving act would set in motion.

All details of crime scene, confessions, and trials were gathered from *The Daily Sentinel,* dated from between August 14, 1937 and April 15, 1939. Since McHolland's trial had been closed to the public, many thanks to the reporters who diligently tried to accurately portray the details surrounding Jeanette Morris's murder. This book could not have been written without these articles.